RAIDING THE HOARD OF ENCHANTMENT

ALSO BY DAVE SMEDS

The Sorcery Within

The Schemes of Dragons

The Wizard's Nemesis

Piper in the Night

Embracing the Starlight

X-Men: Law of the Jungle

RAIDING THE HOARD OF ENCHANTMENT

†

SEVEN TALES OF HIGH FANTASY

DAVE SMEDS

BOOK VIEW CAFÉ PUBLISHING COOPERATIVE

CEDAR CREST, NM

RAIDING THE HOARD OF ENCHANTMENT
Copyright © 2012 Dave Smeds

Book View Café Publishing Cooperative
P.O. Box 1624, Cedar Crest, NM 87008-1624
BookViewCafe.com

ISBN 978-1-61138-381-2

Ebook edition: May, 2012
Print edition: May, 2014

CONTENTS

A SWAIN OF KNEADED MOONLIGHT   7

THE PAGE TURNER   43

THE BEHEADED QUEEN   75

THE ETHERINE ROAD   105

A MORSEL FOR THE PLAGUE QUEEN   117

THE VAPORS OF CROCODILE FEN   143

BEARING SHADOWS   169

A SWAIN OF KNEADED MOONLIGHT

Long ago, silver dripped from a crescent moon. The drops fell upon the land and became the glimmering brides. They were magical women. The great men of long ago won them as consorts—whether by force, seduction, or contract—and sired children upon them.

The brides lingered in the known realms until their children were grown. When their mortal flesh had aged and its grip upon them loosened, they slipped away. Now they are the stars that wander in the skies.

Or so they say.

I know there is some truth in the tales, because the moment I met Lissa, I saw the avatar marks. The color of her irises churned through shades from gold to burnt umber, as though smoke was pulsing in front of a setting sun. Her fingernails appeared to be mother-of-pearl. I admit those details fascinated me as they would anyone. But it wasn't our differences that mattered to me. It was how we were the same.

We were both eight. Both of us had lost our mothers to the cinder pox the year the Silk Coast traders brought it to our shores. And now we were both dwellers under the same roof.

That was a happy time.

Lissa was the ward of Firin, Lord of Osprey Harbor, who had been her late father's friend. She slept in a bedroom she had known since age five. She was free to step out on her own balcony and wait for the fog to roll in and kiss her cheeks. She was able—with an escort—to explore the tidepools north of town or go out sailing on the bay.

I was Wyvva, the scribe's daughter. Of an afternoon, I would visit the chamber where my father composed the lord's bills of lading and copied ships' charts, and he would give me tea and candied lime and ask about my day. Of a morning, I would help Lissa learn the thousand runes of the North, the seven hundred glyphs of the East, and we would practice side by side with our quills and our iron-gall ink.

In the beginning, those lessons were my duty as a servant. They became a pleasure. All Lissa and I had lacked was a best friend, and now that lack was cured.

We played. We laughed. We became inseparable.

But eventually, the world around us turned to shit.

Now we were grown. My father's corpse had long since been heaved from the funeral bluff to join my mother's among the kelp and starfish. Lissa's foster father had gone into debt to his liege lord, the Duke of Mareswold, and been given little choice of what to surrender in payment. To me, Lissa was a sister of the heart. To others, she was a commodity.

Now our life was this tower room, with no view, and every

breath heavy with inland heat. Now, we were in the clutches of a maggot.

In a few minutes, we would meet a man who might, if luck continued to run sour, take her away to a worse place than this one.

"How do I look?" she asked.

Her gown was dark as coffee. That and its cut took attention away from her curves. The wimple concealed her hair. Yet...

"Still worth throwing on a bed, I fear."

She turned green in the gills. I thought she might vomit on me. I stopped adjusting her sleeves and moved to the side. Unfortunately that meant she glimpsed her reflection in the mirror.

She sighed.

We had tried to dim her beauty, but take a butterfly out of the sunlight and it is still a butterfly.

"I truly do not deserve this," she said.

"You truly do not," I replied.

A knock announced the arrival of our escort. Wood grated on metal brackets as the bar was lifted. A heavy key turned in the lock, and the door swung out into the sentry vestibule—in the manner of a dungeon door.

The man in the vestibule was a guardsman named Obber. For all his muscles, he was a eunuch. The duke seldom trusted an intact male with the key to this chamber. I liked Obber. For all his leathers and the crook axe at his side, he was softspoken.

"His Grace summons you."

Had we been able to decline, we would have, but it was no good thrashing against the tide. We thrust our feet into our slippers and strode from our prison, faces smooth, postures stoic.

Then it was down, down, down the steps of the spiral we had come to know too well these past many weeks, Obber clanking in our wake.

"Ah, here we are," I heard the Maggot say as Lissa crossed the threshold into the lord's parlor. "You can see every word I've told you is true."

I kept my eyes on the floor as I slipped into the maid's nook by the door, and Obber into the guard alcove. Once in place, I dared to level my gaze and take in the scene.

The Maggot was in his finest parlor wear, his shoulder cape embellished with gems large and small. He never dressed this way outdoors for fear some of his wealth might slip off and be lost in the mud. His guest was surprisingly shabby by comparison. The latter's ensemble was unadorned and, though made of expensive cloth, looked as though it would hold up on long campaigns spent in the saddle of a warhorse.

"His lordship Count Urley. The lady Lissa of Osprey Harbor." As usual, the Maggot was efficient in his introductions.

The count had perhaps once been handsome. Now his skin was tight against his bones, and creviced from weather, wear, and war. Perhaps when he had been seventeen, admirers might have called him slender. Now he was just gaunt. If he had anyone left who claimed to be admirers, they were remembering a man who no longer existed.

I could say one thing for him. His blood could still flow. He stared at Lissa as would a man half his age. Many who meet her find themselves disconcerted by the mutable quality of her eyes. Urley, however, gazed right back.

And licked his lips.

"Turn around. Let me see the other side," he commanded.

Lissa turned.

"Bend over a bit."

Lissa spun back around. Her spine had already been straight, as those things go. Now it straightened even more. Meanwhile I was trying not to choke on my own spit.

"No need for that," the Maggot told his guest. "Have no fear. I'm sure you'll find her mountable enough, should you make me a serious offer."

"I made an offer. Did it not sound serious?"

"It was inadequate by quite a margin," the duke informed him. "Or do you think an heir to be worth so little?"

"I'll pay more once she's proven herself."

"You can see the Brides' Marks for yourself. Has any woman bearing those signs ever failed to give her husband a son?"

"There's always a first time."

"In that unlikely event, you are free to demand a refund. But until I have payment in full in my treasury, you'll not so much as pluck a hair from her scalp."

They paused to exchange scowls, and Lissa saw her opening. "Your Grace? Do you need me any longer?"

The Maggot didn't bother glancing at her. He just waved his hand in dismissal.

Lissa retreated to the door before he could change his mind. I exited behind her, Obber dutifully ensuring that we headed back to the tower and not to the nearest way out of the castle.

Getting to the top level seemed to sap the last of the strength from Lissa's legs. I supported her by the elbow as we headed for the divan.

I had never seen her as listless and spent as this. But how could she not be, after the previous few minutes?

Obber's gentle comment caught up to us. "Do not fret, m'lady. His Grace won't let that scabby goat have you."

Lissa jumped. She had not realized our escort was still standing in the open doorway. Somehow even with his girth, he had the knack of disappearing from one's view.

Lissa tilted her head. "Will he not?"

"No. The goat's too cheap. Won't offer more than he already has."

I chuckled. How had we missed it? It was plain enough.

The worry lines in Lissa's forehead smoothed out. "Thank you for that, Obber."

"You are most welcome, m'lady." And with that he closed the door. The key turned in the lock, the noise reverberating off the gaps between the tapestries.

—o—

By bedtime, it was clear Obber's assessment had been accurate. No summons had come up ordering Lissa to prepare to leave with the count. Lissa fell asleep at once, making up for the anxious wakefulness of the previous night. She was still asleep as I slipped out of my cubby into the main chamber the next morning.

I poured water from the ewer to the basin and washed my face. I tried to keep my mood high so as to greet my lady with it, but I knew too well the reprieve was temporary. There would soon be another suitor to take the count's place. He would surely be as old. Perhaps older—a greybeard desperate to make an heir while still capable of plowing the furrow. A younger nobleman could afford to select a wife from among the usual candidates, but not so with the ones who came, money in hand, to try to convince the Maggot to grant their petition. A woman who bore the Brides' Marks always conceived easily and always produced a firstborn son. That son bore the peculiar grace of his mother's heritage, and grew up robust, bright, able-bodied, and, if rumor was to be believed, unusually lucky in the face of chance. In short, he was progeny of the sort any lord or king wished to see as his heir. It didn't matter that subsequent children were more often than not female.

Lissa stirred. When I turned, I was surprised to find as radiant a smile on her face as I had seen from her since her foster father had confessed his inability to shelter her any longer.

"What is it?" I asked.

"My deliverer is on his way."

"Your—" I blinked. "How do you know?"

"I have dreamed it."

My insides bounced like sand fleas. This was what I had been fearing would happen. The ordeal had unhinged her mind.

"Um. When is he to arrive?"

"Soon." She brushed away the pillow-tangled hair from her face. Her cheeks were flushed, her lips plump, as if she had just been kissed.

"Wh-who is he?"

She closed her eyes, rolled on her side, and within moments was breathing deeply and regularly.

"Lissa?" I murmured.

She did not respond.

I decided it was best to leave her as she was. She slept soundly for another hour. Then, after a few minutes of tossing and turning, she sat up. Only then did she open her eyes.

She craned her head to gaze through one of the windows that ringed the chamber.

How those windows taunted us. Because summer was upon us, they were unshuttered, yet the ventilation gave us only minimal relief from the heat. The sills were set at half again the height of a man, so we had no view of anything but sky unless we shoved a chest against the wall and climbed upon it. Most of all, the openings gave the illusion that escape was within reach. But no. Even if we had possessed rope with which to rappel down the outer walls, it was a forlorn prospect. Lissa and I were both petite, but we were womanly enough that neither our bosoms nor our hindquarters would fit through such narrow apertures. They were pigeon's gates.

"Shall I ring for breakfast?" I asked, hand poised by the pull cord. I wasn't at all hungry, but at least the question might bring her home to port.

"Four days past full," she said. "That's good."

She was still staring upward. I sat on the bed next to her and was finally able to see what she was looking at. She was facing west. There through the window was a waning gibbous moon, a disc of silver within a rectangle of cerulean.

"Why is it good?" I asked.

She turned to me, as if just realizing I was there. "I don't know." She rubbed grit from her eyelashes. "Was I talking in my sleep?"

"I'm afraid so."

"What did I say?"

I told her.

"A deliverer. Wouldn't that be nice?" She mimed an executioner slitting her throat. Delivering her from this life.

She was her old self. Suddenly I was wistful for the Lissa I had so recently seen. The hopeful one.

"Breakfast?" I repeated.

"Bath first," she said.

"Before calisthenics?"

"No exercise today. I feel as though I spent all night hard at work. I want to do a lot of reading today. *The Tale of the Handsome Bladesman*, I think."

"Don't you know that one by heart?"

"It gets better every time. Don't you think?"

"I do," I admitted, and went to her cedar box to locate the book.

—o—

The day passed slowly, as every day of our imprisonment had. The maidservant who brought our supper let us know the Maggot had departed to visit the king's court. He would be gone four days.

"That's something to cheer," I said as we sat down to the meal.

"No, it's not," Lissa countered. "He'll use his time there to peddle my womb. There's no better place for that than court."

I patted her hand. "Then live in the present? Four days is four days."

She nodded, but without vitality. She ate only the soup and a few bites of bread.

—o—

Some time in the night, I woke with a start. Lissa and I were not alone. I was sure of it.

Heart pounding, I carefully, as surreptitiously as possible, parted the gauze curtain that isolated my sleeping alcove.

A man was standing by Lissa's bed. Moonlight glinted off the hilt of the sword at his belt.

I screamed.

Lissa thrashed and sat up, crying out.

I could not account for what I saw then. The intruder vanished. Not by ducking behind the bed. Not by running away. He had simply ceased to occupy the place he had been standing. The moonglow had been too bright and my eyes too well adjusted to the late hour to blame the effect on dimness.

The bar clanked to the stone floor outside. The key clicked sharply in the lock. Obber burst into the room, his axe in his raised hand. "M'lady? Are you well?"

"Yes," Lissa replied, with a calmness I knew was false but which would fool most who did not know her as well as I did. "It was just a dream."

The guard raised an eyebrow. Lighting a pair of chamber lamps, he made a quick inspection of the wardrobe, my maid's alcove, the privy nook, and the underside of Lissa's bed—the only places in our suite where anyone could be hiding.

He grunted. "Sorry to disturb. Good night."

As soon as he had secured the door behind him, I rushed to Lissa's side.

"Did you see him?" she asked. "The bladesman?"

"I—" Her question made me see what I had missed in the midst of my fright. The silhouette had been that of a lithe man wearing a sword, the hat on his head embellished with a peacock feather.

As in the book.

"Was he handsome?" Lissa asked.

"I...I believe he was," I whispered.

"Then for all that you love me, don't scream next time."

She fell back on her pillow, eyes closing. It was then I realized she had not really been awake.

—o—

In the morning, she said nothing of the incident. I couldn't help but notice, though, that she moved around the chamber with a briskness she had not shown in weeks. Her brow was unfurrowed. She expressed interest in what clothes to put on for the day.

I hesitated to disturb this development with pesky questions, but at lunch I asked, "Your foremother. She had many powers."

"So they say."

"Do you think it's possible you inherited more than you know?"

"You mean, more than the part that makes men want me as their broodmare? More than this?" She held out her hands, displaying the glistening nacre of her fingernails.

"Yes."

"I have no idea. I was so young when my mother died. She had no chance to tell me. Why do you ask?"

"I'll tell you tomorrow," I said.

—o—

That night, I waited until I was sure Lissa was asleep, then I pulled away the gauze curtain and sat on my bunk, watching. The hooting of an owl filtered in through the windows. The air wafting down took on a trace of coolness, though it was inadequate by my harbor-rat standards.

The moonglow began to shine directly into the chamber, and I thought to myself, a waning moon rises at night, so it is always in the sky during the hours before dawn, when dreams are richest.

Lissa's chest began rising and falling as dramatically as if she were engaged in heavy labor. Her mouth opened.

Her breath was visible. Grey mist. With each exhalation, the cloud grew at her bedside. Gradually, the cloud's shade deepened, and its shape grew more defined.

The cloud became the handsome bladesman. Tones of color inhabited his complexion. The metal of his accouterments began to gleam. He became as solid as any real man would be, lacking only motion to seem alive. And then he turned to me, lifting a finger to his lips for silence.

I nodded.

Lissa's breathing returned to normal. No more mist. Yet the bladesman remained. He caressed Lissa's check with the lightest of strokes before he quietly eased away from the bed and approached my alcove.

Gales of the north, he *was* handsome. Suddenly it occurred to me that my nightgown was clinging to my upper body like skin. I pulled the bedsheet higher.

"Who are you?" I asked.

"Do I need a name?" As I had, he kept his voice at low volume—quiet enough not to startle Lissa awake, and quiet enough that Obber would not hear us at all through the thick door and stone walls.

"Of course you do."

"As you wish. Do you have one to give me?"

I hesitated. The bladesman in the story was unnamed, save by description. That had been part of the character's allure. But I wasn't going to have a man in my bedchamber at night without knowing his name. "Vannen," I said. It was the name my father had told me would have been used for my first brother, if my mother had lived long enough to bear a son.

"Vannen it is," he said.

"Why are you here, Vannen?"

"To rescue you." He drew his sword and thrust at the air.

My breath caught. He moved with such sureness I knew he could deliver a lethal blow to an opponent almost before a bout had begun.

"If you are ready, give a scream to draw the guard in, and I will dispose of him."

The thought made me hiccup. "No."

"Eh? I promise you it will be quick. Turn your gaze away, and I will be done before you turn it back."

"You cannot kill Obber," I said. "Kill the duke. Kill the chamberlain. Kill any of those spawn of privy piles that fetched us from Osprey Harbor. But not Obber. He has been kind to us."

Vannen swished his weapon right and left. He held it up to the moonglow. It shone. He had a right to admire it. It was a fine key to unlock our prison. Under other circumstances.

"It would trouble my lady greatly to think her liberty had been won at the cost of Obber's life," I said firmly. "Surely you were not made to bring her such pain."

He sighed. He thumbed the opening of his scabbard, poising the sword to slide it back in.

"You vex me."

"I'm sorry."

"If I am to spill no blood tonight, what am I to do?"

I barely had to think about it. "Spill sweat instead," I said. "Show me your dance."

He cocked his head and gave me a smile. It was just like the smile in the story, the one that made the damsel give up her plan to remain a maiden all her days.

"As you wish," he declared.

He began the dance slowly, displaying the techniques in a way I could follow. Then he repeated them at speed. He thrust. He parried. He charged. He withdrew. I had seen fencing dances before, but not of this level.

Truly, Obber owed me his life.

After a quarter hour, the heel of Vannen's boot happened to bump against the corner of the wardrobe, a sharp thwack of hardened leather against oak. Lissa gave a soft cry and opened her eyes.

Vannen disappeared. A faint haze of mist lingered for an instant, then that, too, was gone.

Lissa lifted her head from the pillow. "What's going on?"

I rushed to her side. "We need to make some plans," I said.

—o—

The next night, Lissa understandably could not fall asleep right away, but ultimately she managed it. Her breath turned silver. Our visitor manifested.

He was just a boy this time. Eleven, perhaps twelve years old. Mature enough to have some strength to him, but with none of the bulkiness of a man's physique. He had a long coil of rope draped over one shoulder.

I was sitting on the divan, the better to watch the magic

occur. As soon as he was capable of movement, he joined me.

His smile was the same as it had been. He was still Vannen, even if he had no beard, no sword at his belt. In some ways, I found him more approachable. Not so intimidating. I put my hand on his knee as he sat down.

"I feel so much lighter this way," he said.

"Well, that is the idea," I replied. I gazed up at the row of windows.

He studied the openings as well, then measured out the width of his hips. "Yes. I think I will fit. Only one way to know."

We moved a trunk against the wall and he hopped onto it. He tied one end of the rope securely to a torch bracket and tossed the coil through a window.

Getting through the narrow aperture took him several minutes. Even if Lissa and I had been as skinny, neither of us could have managed it. Vannen had to twist, hold his body in position with the support of torso muscles alone. He had to grip masonry with supple, strong fingers. He had to somehow keep from falling until he was all the way out and could at last seize the rope properly.

Finally he was suspended above the moat, ready to rappel down and swing to a courtyard or a lower window. Only his head remained visible. In the dimness I made out the white of his smile.

I blew him a kiss.

I could only wait after that, until my yawns torqued my jaw and I had to lie down. At first light I stirred. Vannen was back, worming his way into the tower as laboriously as he had exited. He was puffing and sweating. He almost fell as he got his last leg inside.

I helped him off the table.

"I couldn't get far enough," he reported. "I would have been seen. You would not believe how many sentries there are. What's the Maggot afraid of?"

"Thieves," I said. "He's always thinking about his riches."

"I see. Well, I'll have to try again tomorrow night. Maybe they won't be as vigilant."

—o—

The next night he did not even get as far as the first time. Our plan had several weaknesses. Vannen could not be both a boy slender enough to make it out the window, and a mighty swordsman capable of surreptitiously killing guards all the way up to the top of the tower as he infiltrated the castle. And if he did make it to our door, what of Obber? Slip Obber a sleeping potion? Well, yes, if we had a sleeping potion. Lissa could dream that Vannen had such a thing in his pocket, but how would we get Obber to consume it?

And then the Maggot returned. Later that day, he summoned us. Our first thought was that Vannen had been seen, or perhaps the rope had been spotted dangling from the window. But no, our tormentor was in far too good a humor.

"My time at court was well spent. I have not one, but three wealthy lords prepared to make offers." He rubbed his palms together. "Now I get to play them off each other, until I get the best price possible."

Numb, we said nothing as we climbed back to our chamber. Once there, we silently sat down at our work table and picked up our bead-weaving, resorting to our old standby to keep us occupied with something other than our desperation. The pastime was one of the few bits of Osprey Harbor culture we had been able to bring with us.

"Time is getting short," Lissa said.

"Yes," I mumbled.

"There is one thing we haven't tried. Please know I am serious about it."

"What is it?" By that point, any option was welcome, but her steely tone alarmed me.

"If I were already pregnant, the Maggot would have to stop offering rich oafs the chance to *get* me pregnant."

The bead in my hand slipped free and tumbled noisily off the table. "Wh-, wh-, what are you suggesting?"

"That Vannen lie with me, of course."

"Would that work?"

"If my foremother could become so much a part of this world as to breed with a human man, I don't see why Vannen's seed would not quicken once it's inside me."

"But what about the—you know. Do you think you could stay asleep while...while..."

"While the deed is being done?"

"Yes."

"I will have to find a way." She drummed her fingers on the table. "Tell me, do you think we could convince Obber to sneak us an entire jug of wine?"

—o—

By the time Lissa retired that evening, she was so drunk she needed my help just to make it from the divan to her bed. I helped her get undressed—no nightgown for her tonight—and covered her with a sheet.

Beneath the covering, she flopped her limbs apart so that she was lying spread-eagled. "There," she said, as if she had completed her part, and the goal was all but accomplished. She was snoring in less than a minute.

Hands shaking, I put out the lamps and tapers. I retreated to my cubby and pulled the drape closed. A real drape, not the gauze curtain that normally hung there. Something opaque. I lay back and stuffed cotton in my ears.

I didn't see how I was going to get through the night. I knew perfectly well I wasn't going to be able to sleep, no matter how it might help the cause of discretion.

The plugged ears only made my restlessness worse. I took the cotton out, hoping that if I were comfortable, maybe I would in fact fall asleep. But of course, I was wide awake when I began hearing rustles of movement from the middle of the room and knew that Vannen had materialized.

A soft whoosh told me the sheet had slid to the floor. I tried to banish the vision in my mind's eye of Lissa lying there as Vannen's shadow loomed across her.

The bed creaked as it coped with the addition of his weight. Subtle sounds of movement followed. Was he shifting her? Was he *priming* her? Was he already inside?

A garbled cry raised hair on the nape of my neck.

Suddenly it grew all too quiet.

After a few moments came the sound of a pillow being thrown at the wall. I heard Lissa muttering, and the sound of her pacing back and forth—I recognized the rhythm of her tread. Candlelight began to glow around the edges of the drape. Finally the partition was thrust aside. Lissa stood there in her nightgown, neck stiff, eyes bloodshot.

I didn't ask how far things had gone. Obviously not far enough.

"There's a tiny man inside my skull trying to bludgeon his way out," she whimpered.

"Shall I brew us some sailor-ashore tea?"

"Yes. And next time we get wine, don't bother serving me any. Just hit me over the head with the jug. It will save time."

—o—

The tea leaves were a little stale. Lissa's hangover was still plaguing her in the morning. She was petulant with me even when I was reading from *The Sailmaker's Wife*, one of her favorites. But as the day went on, stage by stage her mood shifted. She lingered in the bath. She stayed in front of the mirror after I had combed her hair, turning her body this way and that. Evaluating.

She dabbed scented oil behind each ear. I tied a ribbon around her neck, crafting the knot just so. After dinner, she chewed fresh mint leaves.

This time she needed no help getting into bed. In fact, she banished me to my cubby even before she retired.

I had promised myself I would fall asleep. I think I may have succeeded. But I snapped awake after midnight, suddenly sure that Vannen was in the tower.

Yes. I heard subtle indications of movement. But no creaking of a bed. In fact, no sound at all from the part of the room where the bed was.

I couldn't stand it. I lifted a corner of the drape and peeked out.

Vannen was sitting on the divan. He beckoned me with a

gesture.

I joined him. "What are you doing?" I asked.

"Waiting. A little later in the night will be better. She's less likely to wake then."

"I see."

He was of course no longer the boy who had squeezed through the window, but he was not quite back to being the bladesman. He was less muscular, less impossibly handsome. Now he was appealing in a grounded way, an honest village man worth marrying and making a family with, not some charmer about to dash off to another adventure.

He smelled like mint.

"She dreams me well tonight. Last night her slumber was impaired."

"We thought the wine would help."

"No, she has to be alert enough to welcome me within her body. Otherwise the penetration is too startling."

I felt a blush coming on. I turned my face away.

"Are you all right?" he asked.

"Yes. I'm fine."

"If it would make you feel better, you might like to know I'm embarrassed by this as well."

I turned back. "You are?"

"I have yet to prove myself in bed. What man wants that? And if things continue to go poorly, I have not one but two women privy to my failure."

"For what it's worth, it's not my idea to be able to know so much. I'd be happy to let it be a secret between the two of you."

"I know."

I waved at the windows. "This would all be simple if she could just dream us far from here, where we were already safe. Beyond the duke's reach."

"If she had that sort of magic, she would not need my help. Are you weary of my company?"

My hand shot to my mouth. "I didn't mean it that way."

"Good. You don't want to make me feel unwanted. I don't think it would help."

"You should never feel unwanted. Until you appeared, the tide was over our heads."

He smiled at me. It was difficult not to blush again.

"What do you think he will be like?" Vannen asked when the pause grew long.

"Who?"

"My son."

"I couldn't say. How could I know?"

"Boys think like their mothers, even if they do it in a male way. You know Lissa. Therefore you know how her son will perceive the world."

I wasn't sure he was right, but I had to admit he had found a way to keep me talking.

He poured what little wine was left into a pair of goblets and we sipped as I spoke of this trait or that, whatever I judged to be the sort of thing the child might inherit.

The child. Somehow he already seemed to exist.

Eventually I had nothing more to say. I closed my eyes. I yawned.

He leaned over to whisper in my ear, "Thank you, Wyvva. I enjoyed this."

I felt myself being lifted in strong arms, to be deposited on my bunk. "Good luck," I murmured as he closed the drape.

He did not approach Lissa's bed while I was alert. It happened some time later, when my pillow had become a chariot to elsewhere, and I could not tell a human sigh from the flutter of a bat's wings.

—o—

At breakfast, Lissa looked incredible. "You're glowing," I said.

"I am not," Lissa replied.

"Are too."

She smiled like wharf pelican. "Maybe you're right."

"You know I'm right."

"Well, it is how I'm supposed to feel, isn't it?"

"Ideally," I admitted.

"I hope it's like this every time."

I almost choked on a piece of melon.

"You did realize we'll have to keep doing this every night until we're sure I'm pregnant?" she asked.

"Your foremother was a glimmering bride. Isn't once enough?"

"Maybe. But I have to be sure."

I carefully swallowed the piece of melon. Lissa stole a second piece from my bowl.

"You really slept through it all?" I asked.

"If I hadn't, 'it all' would not have been possible."

"True."

"It is odd, though, to know I have lain with a man, yet never spoken with him. Thank goodness for you. Tell me what he said last night."

I paused, spoon raised. "We didn't talk. I fell asleep before you did. I slept all night. It's better that way, don't you think?"

Lissa gazed at me so steadily, I lowered the spoon back to the bowl.

"Wyvva. I want to know what he said."

I hated that she knew so immediately whenever I lied. Conceding, I told her how Vannen had asked what traits his son-to-be might inherit, how he had gazed at Lissa so fondly. But I did not tell her how long we had spoken, nor of how he had carried me to my bed, nor of his whisper in my ear.

That part was for me alone.

—o—

True to form, the Maggot could not help but play his prospects against one another as long as possible. Each time he received a better offer, he would summon us to his hall and cackle about it. Finally he intimated that he would probably accept the next one, and told Lissa to air out her best dress.

Meanwhile the nights went on, through the phases of the moon. Lissa's breath no longer had to be anointed by the orb's glow to make Vannen appear. He manifested as soon as she slipped into unconsciousness. He and I had more and more time each night to talk. I was always bleary-eyed in the morning from staying up late; I compensated with naps rather than have to retire when Lissa did.

Each night, he lay with her. We never resumed our conversations afterward; I did not want to sit there while he was fragrant with her scent. I stayed in my alcove.

Sleep seldom came quickly. From time to time, a soft masculine grunt would filter through the partition, or a drowsy feminine sigh. Inevitably, I sometimes could hear other sounds, ones more primal and rhythmic. Wet sounds.

Not once did I nudge the drape aside and peer out, but it hardly mattered. I could see Vannen so plainly in my mind's eye, his hair tousled, the sweat glistening on his shoulders, the muscles of his hindquarters tightening and relaxing. And then his whole body shuddering.

Lissa had always had more than I. But never before had I envied her.

—o—

Finally Lissa began throwing up in the morning. It confirmed what we'd been suspecting for some time.

She sent a note downstairs saying she was pregnant. Within an hour the local birthwitch visited the tower and gave Lissa an examination. The Maggot barely waited until she was done before he burst into the room.

The birthwitch gave the sign of a swelling belly. The duke rounded at Lissa.

"Who did this?" he demanded.

"Count Urley," Lissa said. I nearly coughed out loud to hear her say it so calmly, unable to quench the awful image of that old man climbing into Lissa's bed, even knowing no such thing had ever happened.

The Maggot's mouth dangled open. "Count Ur—"

"He wouldn't meet your price," Lissa added. "But he met mine."

The duke's face purpled to such a degree I thought a blood vessel would pop. "He will not make a fool of me!" He whirled around and stalked from the room, slamming the door.

After Obber had reopened the door and let the birthwitch

out, Lissa and I were finally free to burst into laughter. We muffled the noise as best we could in our sleeves.

It was worth dying now, if we had to.

—o—

That night, I keened my ears for the whisper of Vannen settling onto the divan. When I thought I heard it, I burst from my cubby.

"I have such news—"

The rest of the words lodged in my throat. Vannen was not there. The chamber was empty of anyone except Lissa, asleep in her bed, and me, teetering on the balls of my feet.

There was no reason to continue toward the divan. Chin down, I returned to my bunk.

At first, I told myself the night was young, and I had simply been impatient for him to arrive. But Lissa slumbered on, her exhalations never taking on their magical glow. No version of Vannen, be it bladesman or boy or lover, put in an appearance.

I stayed up until dawn, wondering what sort of good-by I might have composed, if I had known one was necessary. None seemed adequate.

—o—

As the next day wore on, we expected a summons. The need to punish us was surely burning a hole in the Maggot's bowels.

"If it happens, so be it," Lissa said aloud. She was exuding a sort of peace unlike any I had seen from her, even in the happiest portions of our girlhood.

More hours passed. It seemed the duke was reacting as we had thought he might. Inasmuch as we were his captives, he had plenty of time to concoct just the right revenge. At the moment, his anger was directed outward—at the supposed perpetrator of his ills. We had time for developments to fall in our favor.

Hopeful as we were, the form those developments took was a surprise. As evening deepened, a knock came on the door. A few moments later, Obber let himself in.

"Hurry," he said. "His Grace is off to demand satisfaction from Count Urley. He's all but emptied the castle of guards. If you come now, I know I can sneak you out."

"You'd do that?" I asked.

"I would." He waved his thick fingers in the direction of the door. "I have transportation arranged to get you down the road a ways, but you have to be aboard within the hour. Take what you can carry. Nothing more."

We didn't need to hear it again. Lissa and I scurried about the chamber, gathering up necessities. We nearly collided as we both remembered the most important—the purse she'd hidden in a compartment of her cedar box. Wherever we went, gold would help smooth our way.

It felt wonderful to put on footwear meant for the outdoors.

Obber was true to his word. He knew the servants' corridors and the archers' crannies, which together became a route to an unwatched sally port. We were slipping into alleys in the mercantile district in less time than it took for the solitary sentry on the battlements to pace out a full circuit. All we glimpsed of him was the back side of his spiked helmet.

Finally we approached a large wagon. A pair of oxen were already hitched to the yoke. The load was covered by a thick tarp.

Obber lifted the back end of the tarp. A rich aroma of beer

escaped. On the wagonbed was half a load of kegs and barrels.

"Brewmaster is sending this all the way to Rowan Hollow. Load has to go in the cool of the night. His boy owes me a favor. He'll not say a word about carrying any passengers. From Rowan Hollow, you're on your own."

"We'll manage," Lissa assured him.

He grinned. "If I know the old goat, he'll put up quite a fight. His Grace will have to lay siege. Your trail will be cold before he gets the chance to go sniffing along it."

I kissed his cheek.

"We can never thank you enough," Lissa told him. "You are taking quite a risk."

"Worth it," Obber said firmly. "I lost my balls fighting in my master's Ten Valleys campaign. He never thanked me for it."

"How like him," Lissa said.

Obber gazed at Lissa's belly as if able to see a bump there already. "I don't know how you managed it. I've never seen His Grace yank his own beard so hard."

He giggled. It was infectious.

Our eyelashes wet with tears, Lissa and I climbed into the gap between the barrels. Obber gave us one final nod and tied down the tarp over the top of the load, concealing us. His heavy bootsteps faded away.

Soon came the sound of someone climbing onto the driver's bench. A snap of the lash and we were on our way out of the alley and down the street.

The wheels, despite a recent greasing, groaned from the load as the oxen pulled us along, and the barrels, despite being well secured, rattled with each bump. The noise ensured our conversation would not be overhead.

"We can't go back to Osprey Harbor," I said. "They'd look for us there."

"Agreed. We'd only get Lord Firin in trouble. No, we have to leave Mareswold entirely. At night, if we can manage it."

"At night?"

"Assuming I can sleep on the road." She placed her hand upon mine. "Don't you agree it would be prudent to have a male escort?"

"I didn't consider that it was possible."

"You thought me done with him?"

I didn't answer. I was glad she couldn't see my expression in the darkness beneath the tarp.

"With him around, things seem to go well for us. I see no reason not to keep bringing him back as often as possible." She paused. "Do you have some objection to him accompanying us?"

"No," I answered at once. "Not at all."

"Then it's settled. All we need is a destination."

Strange as it may seem, we had never discussed this. Maybe we were afraid to contemplate the endpoint of our escape so completely, and be hurt all the more to be denied it. But now I believed we could make it whatever distance we needed to go. With hope as tangible as that, the answer came to me at once.

"I know a place."

—o—

I awoke to the sound of owls tucking themselves in for the day in the upper recesses of the shack, amid the tangle of myrtlewood branches and thatch. I inhaled air perfumed with the scents of clover and elkbroom. For a moment, I was ten years old again, waking up on this very pallet during the one summer I had spent away from Osprey Harbor.

I rose and parted the curtain that ran down the center of the shack. Lissa, face already washed, already wearing her day dress, was combing her hair. She beamed at me.

"This is a beautiful place," she said.

"It is," I agreed. "Have you seen the ocean?"

"No. It's visible from here?"

"Just up the hill."

"You'll have to show me."

After we breakfasted on cold porridge and blackberries, we climbed up. As soon as we reached the crest of the ridge, the wind thumped us like a family hound left alone all day and eager to show his love.

Off in the distance, blue water stretched to the horizon. We were too far from the shore to hear the waves crash, but we smelled the salt. The pores of our cheeks opened to drink in the moisture. We were inland exiles no more.

Not one human structure intruded upon our view. Not one sail. This stretch of coast was rocky, bereft not only of harbors, but of beaches upon which to pull a fishing boat ashore. It was not a place for lords to covet. Only shepherds saw its value. Of a winter, the winds here blew with fleece-thickening briskness.

We smiled as we took our fill of the scene. But in some ways, the view the other way soothed us just as much. For Lissa, it was the first chance for her to take in the full extent of our surroundings. For me, it was a sweet revisiting. Downslope lay the shack, where a small spring bubbled up, and outcroppings blunted the force of whatever breezes made it down from the ridgetop. A rolling terrain of pastureland stretched inland, the heather interrupted here and there by blackberry brambles, copses of myrtle or ash, and vernal ponds. By a small creek, its outlines hazy with distance, stood the farmhouse from which we had come on foot late the previous afternoon to arrive at the shack at dusk.

The time had come to retrace our steps. We picked our way down the slope and headed hand in hand across the fields toward the house.

—o—

We arrived just as my aunt Nebba was removing the day's batch of bread from the oven. We helped her finish churning the butter and sat down at the table with her and my uncle Foxmo. My cousin Mibb was out with the flocks, but his wife Taney sat with us when she was not having to get up to keep her toddlers out of mischief. The air grew addictively braced with the aroma of fresh loaves breaking open.

"Did you like the little place, m'lady?" Foxmo asked.

"Please call me just Lissa," she replied with cheer. "For now and for good. And yes, I liked it a great deal."

"Be good to have someone out there again full time." My uncle gazed out the window toward the coast. We let him savor whatever memory had bubbled up. I knew he had lived in the shack as a young man. It had been little more than a shepherd's cote back then. He had expanded it when Nebba had become his bride, crafting it into a bower that sheltered them through their newlywed days. But when Mibb was a year old and Nebba pregnant a second time, the old shepherd who had held tenancy of the land had passed away, and Foxmo and Nebba had occupied the main farmhouse, a better accommodation for a growing family. "It's not too isolated for you?"

"Isolation is what we want," Lissa said.

He nodded. "You'll have it. Even the king's tax collectors don't bother coming out this far. We pay our tithe at the village."

As I chewed on warm bread and butter, it seemed to me the most sustaining food I had ever eaten. We had reached a haven where the Maggot's trackers would never look. A bounty hunter clever enough to imagine Lissa and I had sought shelter with my mother's kinfolk would be unlikely to find anyone left alive back in Osprey Harbor to recall what village my mother had come from, and if he did, there was no one left alive in that village who knew to what far-flung corner of the realm Foxmo had drifted off to after he and my grandfather had quarrelled.

The whole way here, I could not vanquish the fear that we might be recaptured in the midst of our flight. Now I could. Now I had.

"We are in your debt," Lissa said.

"Pfff. Won't be long until I am in yours. I met your young man last night. Strapping fellow. Quite an archer. He'll have no trouble helping keep the flocks safe." My uncle pointed to a large pumpkin on the sideboard. The outline of a wolf had been painted on it. The hind half of an arrow jutted from the wolf's heart.

Lissa smiled. She had needed to hear Foxmo say it, for last night, we had suspected him to be a little unsure of us. It was all very well to speak of having a dream man in our service, one who could roam the fields at night, guarding against the predators that regularly swept down along the coast from the north, reducing the number of sheep the pastures would otherwise support. It was another thing to meet the man himself, shake his firm hand, and witness his skills.

"Did Vannen give his own word?" I asked. "Aloud?"

"As a matter of fact, he did." My uncle blinked. "Why wouldn't he?"

—o—

"What was that about? Vannen. Giving his word aloud?" Lissa asked as we stored crocks of olives and rounds of cheese in the root cellar in the hillside near the shack. My cousin Mibb was a full thirty paces away, making repairs to the hen coop so that of a morning, we could have eggs. It was the first time Lissa and I had been alone since we had returned.

I kept my face turned toward the shelves, pretending that wiping dust and cobwebs from the shelves was of greater import than the question. "It occurred to me Vannen might have other plans."

Lissa stayed so quiet I wondered if she had slipped out of the root cellar. I turned around. With the sunlight of the doorway haloing her, I could not read her expression.

"Did he *speak* of other plans?"

"No." I bowed my head. "I just got to wondering. What would some other man want, in his position? If he were just anyone, he might have any number of ambitions."

"He can't have other plans. I *need* him. *We* need him."

"I know. Of course I know. He is as you need him to be. But...is there more?"

She took both my hands in hers. "Wyvva. What troubles you? Tell me."

"Do you remember Frisk?"

"Your father's dog? How could I forget?"

"He was old when we came to Osprey Harbor. My father tried to leave him at a farm, where he would have fields to roam for the last fraction of his life. Frisk wouldn't have it. He wanted to be with my father. He cleaved to him out of love."

"Yes. He did."

"And do you remember that pup Kodder the Innkeeper had, the one we would see by the wharf?"

"Yes. Poor whelp."

"He stayed because he was tied up."

Lissa blanched. "Sister, if you think me evil, I could not bear it."

"When it comes to you, I only ever think of love," I said. "That's how it will be until I'm too old to chew a soup bone. I am like Frisk that way."

She hugged me. "I will do all I can to be worthy of that love."

—o—

Throughout the week that followed, Lissa and I were preoccupied with nesting in. After our months of idling while confined in the tower, it suddenly seemed as though there was so much to do. We ended each day tired, and I slept all the way through most nights. Even when I did wake, I did not see Vannen. Mott was staying up after the rest of us retired in order to instruct him in the places where the flock should be, where wolves or grass panthers might turn up, and then Vannen would roam through the small hours of the night, taking the full measure of the territory that fell within Foxmo's tenancy.

But then came a night when the moon was at its fullest, and my restlessness would not cease. I rose, threw on the sheep-maid frock Aunt Nebba had given me, and slipped out of the shack.

Something whisked by my head, and I blurted an unladylike word.

It fluttered by again in front of me. A hawk moth. It continued on its way out across the fields, and as I tracked it, I saw many more of its kind, travelling in their swooping way, or poising like hummingbirds, or landing upon moorflowers to harvest nectar.

My breath caught at the beauty of it. I had forgotten the moths. Of a moonlit night in late summer or early fall, waves of them flowed over the heather like sea foam.

Over on the crest of the nearest knoll I made out Vannen's tall shape. He had one hand poised on an unstrung bow, the other hand holding up a sprig of elkbroom. A moth settled upon the sprig to feed. He bent his head to study the patterns of its wings.

I followed the path down from the shack and then up the gentle slope of the knoll, keeping alert for gopher holes and stones that might be hidden in the pasture's verdant mat.

Vannen watched me approach. With his face in shadow, I did not see how wide his grin was until I got close.

"You're in a happy mood."

"Your aunt left me one of her mutton pasties. And a cup of her cider. It was wonderful."

It was the emotion in his tone that made me realize, worldly as he might have been in other respects, he had never before eaten.

"She doesn't need to waste food on me," he added. "But I won't be the one to tell her so."

"Then neither will I."

He held out his bow to me. "Hold this, please."

After I had taken it from him, he ambled to the nearest

clump of elkbroom, and headed back with a fresh sprig in his hand. A dirt clod crunched beneath his foot. Where he had stepped, the grass remained crumpled. He was solid. The things he did had an effect on the world. It did not seem possible that when Lissa woke, he would vanish.

I ran a finger along the bow. Fine yew, well crafted. As far as I knew, it materialized with him each night. If I took it with me to the shack, would it still be there in the morning?

"What are you, Vannen?" I finally dared ask. "Are you only her dream?"

His brows rose. He grew very still as he pondered.

"More than that, I think." He spoke softly so as not to disturb the especially handsome moth that had found his offering. "I suspect that I am not made, but taken from some other place and reshaped. But if I have another existence, I do not remember it while I am here."

"Doesn't that trouble you?"

"Do you mean to ask, am I content?"

"Yes."

He gestured at the silvered expanse of terrain, at the moths in flight. He drew breath until his chest broadened. "When I am here, I know I exist. I smell the heather. I hear the sheep bleat. I have a purpose and the skill to pursue it. So, the answer is yes. I am content. I would rather be alive than not. I am grateful for all that I have."

His voice mesmerized me. Its timber. The sincerity in its tone.

"I will tell Lissa you said so. She will be glad."

I toyed with the loose bowstring.

"There is one thing I want," he added.

I looked up. My mother's ghost watch over me, when I saw

his eyes again it was all I could do not to untie my frock, place it on the ground as a blanket, and invite him to share it with me. "Yes?"

"I am lonely, of a night," he said. "I would have you join me more often. I would like to know you much better, Wyvva Scribe's Daughter."

I hiccupped. "I...I could only do that if Lissa has dreamed it."

He chuckled. "Silly girl. Of *course* she has dreamed it."

Suddenly I was having to wipe wetness from my eyes, and my heart began thundering in my chest.

Vannen removed his quiver of arrows from his back and rested it on the grass. With a nonchalant stride, he halved the distance between us.

I halved the rest. And kissed him.

THE PAGE TURNER

Their route took them south through the borderlands, an empty swath of rock, heather, and fen, spotted with oak and laurel but elsewhere a domain of field mice and hawks. Families had worked some of the fertile spots before the plague years and the war, but only hedgerows and tumbledown chimneys revealed where their steadings had been.

Hyacinth did not like the isolation. For all of her twelve years she had been a village girl, waking to the sounds of carts rumbling to market down the lane beside the tavern, going to sleep serenaded by the murmur of local folk making merry in the common room. Except for Uncle Rowan, the only living person she had seen in the past two days was a greybearded puppeteer trying to get his ox to continue down the trade road.

"Try these," Rowan had said, giving the old man a handful of snap beans. The puppeteer had broken open a pod in front of the ox's nose and the beast had moved forward to eat it. And had kept moving from the promise of more.

"My thanks," the puppeteer had called. And that was the last conversation Hyacinth had heard these last many hours.

Uncle Rowan didn't like the isolation, either. He kept looking back at the way they had come. He studied every thicket they passed by. Once, Hyacinth saw a blur of movement in the shade of a willow. Rowan's hand darted to his sword hilt. But then a rabbit burst from cover, pursued by a meadowcat.

Sometimes Rowan simply stopped and listened. Hyacinth gradually saw the pattern. He did it whenever the birds and insects fell silent. Her heart pounded hard against her breastbone each time it happened, but then a lark or a frog would begin chirping and Rowan would shrug and continue down the road.

Sometimes they rode the mare. Most of the time they walked. Hyacinth's calves were so sore by late afternoon her uncle agreed to make camp early.

As they left the road, Rowan wiped away their tracks and tossed a bit of brush down in their wake, obscuring the path they were taking. They weaved through a sparse verge of oaks until they were well out of sight of any would-be passersby. They did not make their campfire until dusk had faded into a darkness full enough to hide the smoke they made.

The pursuers found them anyway.

Hyacinth was awake when it happened, as always finding it hard to stay asleep with dew forming on her eyelashes. She had risen, emptied her bladder, and returned to the warmth of her bedroll. She watched the stars fade out and was wondering if the sun would ever appear over the horizon when the mare nickered.

Hyacinth turned in the direction of the road and saw the two swordsmen—one skinny, one burly—trying to inch nearer. They were downwind but as Rowan had said, the mare was a skittish nag and she must have sensed the wrongness in the air.

Rowan was suddenly moving. He threw off his blankets and rolled to his feet. By the time he got there his sword was in his hand.

"Do as I taught you," he told Hyacinth.

She scurried from beneath her covers and sprinted away from the strangers. She did not stop until she was past the second large oak—far enough that if she were chased, she could stay ahead.

Back at the campsite, the smaller assailant frowned and ceased circling toward her. Both sides knew now how it would go. It was two swordsmen against one, and only when that was resolved would Hyacinth's fate be known.

Rowan used the terrain to best advantage, positioning himself so that his attackers would have to navigate half-buried boulders and a rotting log in order to come at him.

The pair tried to surround him, but Rowan shifted about so that the burly man was always in the way of the other. Hyacinth had seen her uncle practice these dances; he could keep it up a long time. The attackers soon were beginning to pant. The big one had the muscles and the scars of someone used to wading in and finishing an opponent quickly. The small one kept darting forward and back like a man used to kills of stealth, not engagement. They realized the strategy he was using and stopped working so hard to chase him. That's when Rowan took the fight to them. He flung out his left hand, and dirt went flying into the burly man's eyes. He must have scooped it up when he had risen, but had held it so long his enemies had forgotten he might have anything in that hand.

One thrust, and the burly man had a hole in his throat. He gurgled, blinked through the dirt, and staggered back. He tried to keep his sword up, but Rowan's weapon had punctured a critical spot. The man collapsed to his knees, face going pallid, mouth hanging open.

Meanwhile, Rowan pressed the skinny man hard. The latter parried, stepped back, parried again, tried a swipe at Rowan's legs. He could fence after all. But he moved with sudden jerks, not the smooth, intentional dance Rowan used. Soon his heel caught on a rock, and he stumbled.

Rowan's sword plunged into an upper thigh, right next to his groin. The skinny man yelped and pranced back.

Rowan did not pursue. He caught his breath, waiting for his opponent's next move.

Blood flowed profusely around the skinny man's hand as he held it cupped to the crease of his thigh. Hyacinth saw his expression transform as he acknowledged the mortal nature of the wound.

Meanwhile the burly man finally flopped over, having spent his last moments quietly murmuring. The skinny man's reaction was the opposite. He screamed and rushed in, blade flashing.

Rowan retreated three steps, then held his ground. It all happened so fast Hyacinth didn't catch the details, but suddenly her uncle's sword was protruding out his attacker's back, and he was holding the fellow's sword wrist in a tight grip, keeping the steel pointed away.

The skinny man collapsed limply to the ground and did not move again.

Rowan stepped into the clear and scanned every direction,

first quickly, then slowly and methodically. He beckoned Hyacinth to him. She obeyed, so shaky in the knees she could hardly walk.

"Bind my hand, will you?" he asked.

He held out his guard hand. Blood dripped from a slice on the side of the palm.

Hyacinth fumbled as she fetched a washcloth from her uncle's pack and moistened it with water from her flask. Her hands were only slightly steadier as she cleaned the cut. The injury was small and she knew it would probably heal quickly, but she began to sob anyway, realizing if he had been just a little slower or a little less adept, he would have been hurt far worse.

She wrapped a bandage around his hand and tied it off.

"Well done," he said.

The mare was agitated, trying to edge away despite its hobbles. Rowan took hold of the bridle and lowered the animal's head, forcing her to stillness. He murmured softly in her ear. When the beast had grown quieter, he handed off control to Hyacinth.

The girl opened her mouth, but Rowan held a finger to his lips.

Hyacinth swallowed the question she had been about to ask, and did her best to quiet her breathing.

Rowan moved toward the campfire and stood in the midst of the clearing. He tilted his head this way and that, presenting his ears to every direction.

The burly man's neck was still oozing. A red stain was expanding beneath him, the blood coming too fast for the soil to absorb it all. Hyacinth tried not to be aware of it.

Finally her uncle relaxed. "I'd say that was all of them for now." He wiped his sword off on the burly man's tunic and restored it to its scabbard.

Now that she knew the fight was truly over, the last of her fortitude drained away. Tears began pouring down her face.

Rowan embraced her, letting her weep against his chest. She would have stayed there for an hour, but finally he moved her back to arm's length.

"We need to get away from here."

She nodded. She wanted very much to do exactly that. She stumbled over to the mare and groped for the saddle horn.

"No, we will walk," her uncle said.

"Sh-shouldn't we go as fast as possible?"

"We might need to go fast later, and I want her as fresh as possible."

They set out across open country, avoiding the road. Eventually they came to a creek. The water was no deeper than fetlock height in most places, and the streambed was mostly gravel. At last they climbed into the saddle and rode the mare down the channel. The water rinsed away the signs of their passage. They chose a sunny rock outcropping at which to clamber back onto land. Hyacinth glanced back before they slipped into the riparian brush and saw that the hoofprints were already beginning to evaporate.

No matter how much she tried, she couldn't banish the images of the attackers sneaking into the camp. With every step— they were once more travelling on foot—she calculated how far she was from the spot, and the measure was never enough.

—o—

At sunset they finally came to a farmholding that was not

entirely a ruin. A few charred timbers and barrel staves jutted from the rubble where the barn had once been, but the farmhouse was standing. Weeds and wildflowers rose as high as the shuttered windows and the thatched roof was sagging, but the place was far more inviting than the midge-ridden bog they had just fought their way through. There even a nice long verge of unharvested barley along the paddock for the mare to nibble.

Rowan reconnoitered around the entire farmhouse in his usual cautious way. He was almost smiling as he came back around and pushed open the door. An owl burst from a hole in the thatch up near the crown, setting Hyacinth's heart to racing but having no apparent effect on her uncle. She followed him inside.

Whatever rodents had escaped the owl had left their droppings all over the floor and sideboard, but the walls were still sound and the holes in the thatch above were minor. Enough firewood lay stacked in a corner to see them through the night.

Rowan smiled. "More than this and we'd grow spoiled. Make it cozy for us while I see to the mare." He waved at the raised hearth in the center of the room.

Hyacinth got the blaze going, but then found reasons to putter about outside, needing to be where she could see her uncle. He was giving the mare a thorough rubdown. The beast had coped with the full day of unrelenting travel without going lame, but she needed the care.

Hyacinth drew up water from the well. The frayed rope groaned, barely strong enough to serve, and the bucket leaked, but she knew she was lucky to have the use of them. If they'd been in better condition the farmholders would have taken them as they had nearly every other portable item. She filled their camp kettle and set some porridge to simmering, but justified another session outside by investigating the garden next to the paddock. Gophers had thoroughly colonized the area, but before the twilight deepened too much for her to work, Hyacinth managed to harvest an armful of carrots and a pair of onions. She rinsed them off near the well.

At some point in the domestic routine, she actually managed to concentrate upon the immediate moment, the first time all day that she had not dwelled on the danger they were in. Later, with the floor swept, the house warm, and a soothing fullness in her stomach, she could finally speak coherently.

"Those weren't just highwaymen, were they? They were hunting us. Hunting you, I mean. Why?"

Her uncle seemed to wilt. His expression was hard to read in the firelight, the departed farmsteaders having taken every last candle or lantern with them when they had left.

He sighed. "They wanted the book."

"The one you read every day?"

"I have no other."

The same could be said of almost anyone. Books were for schools, for monasteries, for the king's record houses. Or as in the case of those Hyacinth herself had read, the sitting room of the inn in which she had been raised. Few individuals possessed a book of their very own.

"What is so unusual about it that men would die trying to steal it?"

Rowan had been honing his sword when she had asked her question. He resumed running the whetstone along the blade. As his hesitation went on she became aware of how little she could do to force an answer from him. There he was with his corded strength and ease of movement and his glistening sword, and here was she, a stick of a twelve-year-old girl, her toughness limited to her knees and palms, callused by scullion chores.

He spoke with a seriousness as deep as when he had informed her father he was taking her with him, rather than letting her be subject to his neglect.

"The fewer who know what the book is, the better for everyone," Rowan said. "But you are to travel with me now, so it is only right that you should see for yourself."

He put down his whetstone and sheathed his sword, his actions smooth as oil. From his saddlebag he removed the item of which they spoke. It was already familiar to her from a distance— bound in faded brown leather, the edges of its pages stained and chafed from handling.

He cleared the remains of their meal from the broken stool they had used as their table. He lay the book down where the firelight was good enough to make out its features. It had no embellishments. No gold leaf on the spine. The leather was undyed. It struck Hyacinth as designed for travel and daily use, like a journal or book of meditations, small enough to fit in a large vest pocket. The title, tooled across the face by an unsubtle hand, said simply, "A Life." There was no author's name.

"You can only read a short sample, and only as I direct. You will look only at the part I tell you to. Swear it."

"I swear it. I will do exactly as you say."

"It will be harder than you think," he warned, but he moved back. She knelt by the stool.

She reached out and touched the volume. It was strangely

warm. The flesh of her fingers and palms tingled, as if something were being drawn out of her. She wondered if she wanted to do this after all.

"You will see one leaf, somewhere in the middle, that juts out a bit, not as well trimmed off as the rest. Don't go past that. Choose a spot a few pages before it."

She could see what he meant. Despite the obvious wear and tear on the outside surfaces, the binding was still tight, and the one loose leaf called attention to itself. She put her finger a few pages earlier and opened the book. It was so well crafted it lay flat and open with no need for her to hold the halves apart.

Even in the weak light the words were clear and unmistakable, as if wrought by a scribe.

Hyacinth huddled in the corner as the gravedressers finished their work, arms wrapped around her knees. She was required to witness the cleansing and shrouding, but down here, low on the stone floor, she was able to avoid confronting her mother's face straight on.

Her mother really was dead. And that morning, her father really had appeared from his den down by the wharfs, nearly a stranger given how few times she had ever seen him in the course of her childhood, saying she must live with him now. To clean his house? To be hired out to sailors for...other purposes? Certainly it was not to see to her needs, but only to further his own.

The gravedressers laid a pair of lilies crosswise over the heart that had stopped late the previous afternoon. Three times in as many years Hyacinth's mother had withstood the harbor fever, but not this year, not after it had already weakened her.

The elder of the two attendants laid a hand gently on

Hyacinth's head as she went out. They were not lingering to make sure Hyacinth stood up to examine their work, and say her farewell. They trusted her to do as ritual required.

Hyacinth knew she would do so. In a little while. When she could remember how to make her legs work. Her mother deserved it, and Hyacinth would manage somehow.

But all she could think of right then was what kind of poison to put in her father's porridge. Better to be a full orphan. Only then would there even be a possibility her own survival might come to something worthwhile.

She slammed the book shut. "Who wrote this?" she demanded, her voice going shrill. "You? How could you know?"

Hyacinth had told no one she had wanted to kill her father. By the time of the burial itself the urge had vanished into the fog of her grief. By now she had almost forgotten the incident completely. She was ashamed to have had the impulse.

Her uncle took the book from the stool and set it in his lap. "I did not write it. I did not even read it. You alone know what it said. The book is different for everyone."

"How can that be?"

"No one really knows. The sorceress who created it died long ago. All I can tell you is, the words appear. If I am the reader, the book contains the story of my life, from birth to death. If you are the reader, it is your chronicle. If you had read the first few pages, you would have been reading about your time as a baby."

She blinked. Gradually her heart ceased thundering against the inside of her sternum. The words on the page had left her feeling so naked it was hard to believe she had not been exposed.

Her uncle ran his fingers across the leather cover. "Some men chase me so they can know the parts of their lives they have yet to live. Others are drawn by greed, intending to sell the book to the highest bidder. But the real problem is that more than one mage imagines he or she might be able to decipher the enchantment. They have ways of finding me."

"How many times have you had close calls like this morning?"

"Not many that close," he admitted. "I'm good with a blade, but the key to survival is not to let them catch up to begin with. I'm not used to travelling with a companion. We'll have to get you your own horse."

"Why don't you just give them the book?"

He tapped his chest. "As long as I keep it, I know it is not in the hands of someone who would use it wrongly."

"If that's what you're worried about, why not just destroy it?"

"Some have tried to do that very thing," he said. "I'll give you an idea what happened to them. Stand over there behind the woodpile."

She did as he asked.

"Now pay careful attention, and be prepared to duck if you need to."

She nodded.

He tossed the book onto the fire and retreated as fast as he could.

Before the book could even begin to be scorched, it flew from the fire, spinning tornadolike in a circuit around the hearth, each page edge razoring the air. If Rowan had not backed away fast enough, his skin would have been flayed to ribbons.

The book stopped whirling. It settled gently to the floor.

When Rowan came forward to pick it up, Hyacinth gave a start, fearing would turn back into a weapon, but it showed no sign of that. Soon it was tucked away in the saddlebag.

Rowan used a stick and a broken dinner platter to collect the embers the violence had left scattered over the earthen floor. Hyacinth came out from behind the woodpile.

"There is probably some means to get around the protective charm, but I've never troubled myself to find out how. I've no wish to destroy the book," he said. "It's a work of art unlike any in the world."

It was the worst thing he could have said. It left her feeling as sick as when she had watched the blood flowing from the burly man's neck. "If you don't get rid of it, if you don't destroy it, then we'll never be safe. *I* will never be safe."

He reached out as if to squeeze her shoulder to comfort her, but she retreated. It was his bandaged hand—another reminder of the danger they were in.

She should have stayed with her father.

"I promise you it will be all right," he said.

She didn't believe him. It was the sort of thing men said. She had thought her uncle was a better man than that.

—o—

In the morning they departed along the overgrown lane that led past other abandoned farms. Eventually the lane merged with a dray track that showed signs of recent use. On the other side of a small creek, the route forked, Rowan paused to contemplate the choice.

"That way," he said.

Before long they spotted smoke rising from a chimney in the distance to their right, and then another such plume in the distance to their left. The breeze lavished them with the fragrance of new-cut hay.

The road forked again. This time Rowan chose without hesitation, as if able to read some kind of roadmarker invisible to Hyacinth.

The choice took them over a low wooded ridge into a valley of well-tilled fields. At midday they came to a large holding. They were met by a strapping farmer in a blacksmith apron, forge tongs in his grip, his equally strapping sons and five alert sheepdogs observing from near the house and barn.

Rowan held up a copper eight-bit. "Good day," he called cheerfully. "May we buy some eggs and milk from you?"

The man nodded. "For two of those, you can lunch with us as well."

"Done," Rowan said.

Throughout the meal, the man and his sons chatted amiably with Rowan, asking for news of the north. The food the goodwife placed on the table was filling and good—it was obvious how the men of the family had become so robust. Even the dogs were appealing in the way they begged for scraps. Yet Hyacinth stayed tense until the farm was an hour behind them.

They stopped at a spring where the mare could drink her fill. Rowan washed out his bandage and cleaned his hand. The cut was healing well.

He joined Hyacinth where she waited in the shade, her back propped against a smooth boulder. He chucked her fondly under the chin. "You see. Things are getting better already."

She frowned. One good stopover. A nice meal. Some shade. It would take a lot more than that to make her feel better about having to always be on the run. But the full belly was soothing. Before long, she was dozing. When she woke, she found that her uncle was reading. When he saw that she had opened her eyes, he closed the book and returned it to the saddlebag.

"Ready to go?"

She nodded.

Late in the afternoon they came to a river. They hesitated at the ford, knowing that if they crossed, there were not enough hours of sunshine left to dry their clothes. Hyacinth wanted to do it anyway if only to put another obstacle between them and whatever pursuers might be following.

Around a bend in the stream came a barge. Its sail hung slack, useless while the wind was blowing over the prow. While a matron held the tiller, a trio of middle-aged men—her brothers, based on the similarity of their features to hers—strained at the poles, trying to further their progress upstream. All three were dripping sweat and their hair hung like mop strands.

Rowan called out to them. "Current's running fast this season."

"Aye," the woman called back. "Too much rain."

An hour later, Rowan and Hyacinth and the mare were passengers, the barge making good headway, his manpower at a fourth pole more than enough to make up for the added weight.

Hyacinth felt sure their throats would be slit that night as they lay anchored, but in fact, thanks to her state of exhaustion and the lulling effect of the river motion, she had as profound a night of sleep as she'd had since her mother died. And the breakfast the matron served was delicious. The woman had a trader's grasp of multiple styles of cooking and did not stint on portions, grateful as she was for Rowan's contribution to their progress.

About noon of their third day on the barge, they pulled in at the wharf of a town. They helped the family unload about a quarter of their cargo of tobacco leaf and hempen ropes, and while the matron and her merchant client were occupied haggling with the dockmaster over the tariff, Rowan examined the town with the peculiar concentration Hyacinth had seen in him a dozen times in the past fortnight.

"I believe we'll stay on the barge another few days," he said. "I'm sure we would be welcome."

Hyacinth gazed longingly at the inn she had spotted tucked amid the warehouses. She could smell the familiar aroma of harvest pudding and ale. Drying linens were waving in the breeze on clotheslines in the alley.

"It's not your mother's inn," Rowan said softly.

"Will we ever stay somewhere like that?" she asked.

"From time to time. But not 'til winter comes."

She sighed.

They continued along the river until the barge reached its furthest-upstream port of call. Rowan's muscles were not needed for the downstream run, so he and Hyacinth and the mare debarked amid warm thanks from their companions.

They journeyed next through the hill country. Rowan bought a pony at a tin-mining outpost. It left his purse all but empty, but that was cured when he hired himself out as a guard and scout for a caravan headed across the Ash Waste.

As the days went on and they remained safe, the tightness in her gut eased. When the kettlewives told their jokes at the evening fires, she laughed. When the convoy traversed the shoulder of the volcano that gave the region its character, she was grateful to see for herself how the mountain impaled the clouds and hear for herself how it rumbled like a footsore ox, as in the stories she had heard at the inn as a little girl.

She grew accustomed to seeing her uncle leaning against a wagon wheel during midday breaks, reading the book. He only interrupted the routine if doing so would keep others from getting a close look at the volume.

Just what was he reading? Had he known they would be safe on the barge, and at the mining outpost, and on the caravan? Was the book his guide?

Then why had they been attacked that one time? Hadn't the book warned him it would happen? Maybe it had. Maybe it had once contained a version of their tale in which they were killed, but because he had been forewarned, he had managed to alter their journey just enough that they were attacked at a slightly different time and place, and as a result, they had survived.

That would mean it was possible to change whatever future the book contained. And if that were true, he might *make a mistake*, and transform a harmless occasion into something horrible.

Once she allowed that prospect to incubate, away went the trace of serenity she had been enjoying. And then her anxiety mounted as high as ever when the caravan arrived at its destination, the great port of Crag Bay.

How could so many people exist in one place? And all of them strangers.

Rowan collected his pay and stabled the horses so that they could explore the sights, and soon she was being whisked in his wake, threading across a vast market plaza through a human beehive. The melon vendor by the fountain was shouting his prices so loud it made her ears ring. They were trapped for a dozen paces behind an old woman who smelled like sewage. Hyacinth's elbows and hips were bumped again and again. Worse still, she was sure some of the passersby, especially the leering old fellow with the missing teeth, had made contact on purpose.

"Spice dumplings!" Rowan cried. He angled sharp left toward a food pavilion and into a miasma of alien scents.

"I haven't had these in years," her uncle proclaimed. He placed his order. The cook, a woman adorned in an apron as exotic as her ingredients, handed him fifteen petite dumplings on a platter of banana leaf. He waved them in front of Hyacinth as if they were treasure.

"What's in those?" she asked.

"Cabbage. Spices. And some meat."

"What kind of meat?"

He tossed one in his mouth, chewed, and smiled. "*Good* meat."

"You say that now. What if it *hadn't* been?"

"Then I would have been disappointed."

Eventually he got her to try some. She had to admit as dumplings went, they weren't bad, though one of the spices was so bracing it scoured the road dust from her nose. She still worried what kind of meat she was allowing in her stomach.

He insisted they spend further time perusing the wares of the many booths. At one, he bought a new saddle blanket, but mostly it seemed he was simply enjoying the variety of merchandise, the examples of real craftsmanship, and the enthusiasm of the huckstering. They watched the tumblers and jugglers and clowns. They listened to musicians, some of them playing instruments Hyacinth had not only never heard played before, but never heard described.

"Wasn't this a good day?" Rowan asked.

"I don't like this city."

"What's not to like?"

"I'm tired," she said in the beseeching tone she had learned he would take seriously.

"Very well," he replied. "But it's late. We'll spend the night."

"Where?"

"The loft at the stables will be good enough for us. I've already spoken with the liveryman about it."

They wound their way back to the caravan district where they had left their animals. Hyacinth became disoriented in the maze of streets and alleys, but her uncle led with confidence, and finally the stables appeared at the end of the lane. How did people keep track of themselves in such a place as this?

A drowsy stableboy let them in. They headed deep inside. Hyacinth estimated the building might contain two hundred stalls. That made it larger than any structure of her home village, yet she had seen others larger still over the course of the day.

The mare and the pony were housed near the end of an aisle. She slid into the lead, eager to be with something familiar. As she passed the empty stall where they had left their gear, she immediately noticed that the puzzlelock had been torn off her uncle's saddlebag and the flap was hanging loose.

Something bumped into her. Hard. She went tumbling and ended up prone on the hardpacked floor with a mouthful of straw and something heavy on top of her.

Her uncle moaned and she realized he was the heavy thing on top of her. She pushed with knees as well as arms and managed to roll him off.

A stout, black-bearded man loomed above her, wielding an ox yoke. The end of the yoke was bloody, as was the back of her uncle's head.

Black Beard swung at her. She rolled. The blow landed on the place she had just vacated. The impact sent a shock up the piece of wood. Black Beard grunted.

During the lull as the big man was reasserting his grip, a lasso settled around his neck. His eyes went wide. He dropped the yoke and reached toward his throat, but he was too slow. He was flung back, his legs flipping high. Stable muck flew from the soles of his boots into the rafters. He landed on his head.

Hyacinth let go of a breath she had sucked in when she saw the yoke swinging down at her. The head liveryman burst into view, pulling his hoof trimmer from his belt and cocking it to use against Black Beard if he offered more trouble.

But Black Beard lay without moving. The liveryman frowned, bent down, and removed the lasso. The assailant's head flopped limply to one side. His eyes were open and unblinking.

"I didn't mean to yank so hard," the liveryman said huskily. "But I couldn't let him hit you, girl."

"You did well." The voice was Rowan's. Hyacinth whirled and saw that her uncle had raised up to his elbows.

The liveryman sighed. "He had it coming, I suppose. I don't

imagine I'll lose sleep over it." He stood. "Shall I fetch a healer for you?"

"I'll be fine." Rowan winced as he said it, but his voice was calm and steady. "I must have heard him swinging. I avoided the worst of it."

"I'll bring some cold well water and a washcloth, then."

"Thank you, yes."

With a scowl at the dead man, the liveryman headed off.

Hyacinth helped her uncle to sit up.

"Well," he said, rubbing the back of his head, "that was exciting. He'll have quite a tale to tell to his grandchildren someday, about how he saved our lives."

Exciting? Hyacinth's eyes went wide. "You *liked* it! You thought it was *interesting!*"

His brow furrowed. "I didn't mean it that way." He held out his palm, displaying the smear of blood from the gash in his scalp. "I didn't *want* this. But it's over and we're all right. Should we not savor the good half?"

"There is no good half!"

"Hyacinth..."

She wouldn't listen to any more. She slid into the pony's stall and put the beast between her and her uncle. The blond sorrel tell-no-lies face was the only one she wanted to look at.

—o—

Rowan wanted to retire early to the loft but the liveryman would have none of it, saying that someone who has been knocked out by a blow to the head should be kept awake for several hours, a piece of wisdom passed down within a family whose members had been kicked by livestock more times than they cared to count. The man's wife brought bread, olives, and a wedge of cheese and the liveryman and three of his older stableboys settled in with Rowan in the tack room for a game of pegs and dice, intending to keep it up until midnight.

The group included Hyacinth in their activities. She happened to like pegs and dice, but it was a game favored by males. She quit early, realizing she could create an opportunity if she pretended to be bored.

"I'm going to visit the pony," she said.

"Very well," her uncle replied. So far he had let her sulk in peace. She was counting on that.

She waited just out of sight until the men's game and conversation resumed. Then she sneaked back, and while the others were preoccupied, she went to her uncle's vest, which he had hung from a hook by the doorway after cleaning the blood from it. She pilfered A Life from the pocket. The book had been in the vest all day, not the saddlebag, otherwise Black Beard would not have been obliged to wait around to ambush them.

She retreated to the empty stall where they kept their gear, glad that the city watch had hauled away the body of Black Beard.

She cradled the book in her lap. In its final pages was the answer she needed. Would she grow old and die asleep in her bed? Would she be slain tomorrow? Just what would happen to her?

She turned the book on its face and raised the back cover, exposing the last page.

It was blank.

She hiccupped. She leafed back four, five, six pages. Twelve, fourteen, sixteen. They were all blank.

Suddenly her uncle's arm reached past her and flipped the book shut. She yelped.

He set the book aside, made her stand up, and turned her toward him. She expected him to be scowling. Instead he clasped her hands in his and gazed steadily into her eyes.

"You mustn't. No good will come of knowing." His tone was pleading, not scolding.

"Th-th-the pages were blank." She hiccupped again. "What does it mean?"

"To fill the book to the very last page, you would have to live a very long time. More than a hundred years. Apparently you will die younger than that. At eighty, let's say. Or ninety."

Or twelve? she wondered.

"Promise me you'll never try to read it again."

She hesitated.

"Promise me, Hyacinth. This magic will only burden you. Leave it to me to turn the pages. The book and I—we have an understanding."

"All right," she said. "I promise it, if you will tell me this much. Will I ever be safe again? Will I be happy?"

"Yes."

She blinked. "Yes?"

"Yes," he repeated.

"Do you swear we will have as few adventures as possible?"

"I swear to do my best," he said.

She believed him. If there was one useful thing that had happened in these past few weeks, it was that she had now spent enough time with her uncle to know him better. She was certain he was telling the truth.

"But Hyacinth," he added. "Life is like the weather. No matter what I may do—no matter what you may do—from time to time storms will blow."

—o—

Hyacinth was seventeen years old the spring she and her uncle arrived in Many Mills, a town in the green-wooded, soft-backed hills of King Broadarm's domain.

Their first stop was on the outskirts of town at a saddler smithy, where Rowan ordered new sets of horseshoes. Their mounts were feisty and young and had a tendency to throw shoes. "Find us an inn," Rowan told her as he waited by the forge.

Hyacinth walked along the river to the heart of the town on her own. She liked that he had taken to letting her make such choices. She was, after all, the one who knew just how an inn should be run and had long since proven to him that of the two of them, she made the best evaluations.

Three local young men gazed at her admiringly as she passed by the crossroads fountain. She gave them a warm smile. They smiled back, but did not follow her. Good. Her uncle had schooled her well in defense skills, but she hated having to resort to them.

Five years back her uncle would never have let her out of his sight. After the attack in Crag Bay, thieves and assassins had continued to sniff out their whereabouts no matter where they went. She wore a knife scar on her left arm from the narrowest of their escapes. But two years after Hyacinth had begun to travel with her uncle, a certain sorcerer of the City of Spires had died— killed by a rival of lesser skill but better luck. At first Rowan and Hyacinth had not known this event might have meaning to them, but eventually they noticed the pursuit had become less intense at precisely that juncture. The magician had apparently been their greatest nemesis. With him gone, no other existed powerful enough to pinpoint the book's location unless the artifact remained in the same place for a season or more. Rowan and Hyacinth no longer needed to keep moving so unceasingly. If they found a pleasant situation, they would remain in place for a fortnight or two.

She came to a large mill. The river ran fast, clear, and deep here, supplying plenty of power. Woodsmen brought timber from every direction to be made into lumber in Many Mills. The king shipped in grain from the heartlands to be rendered into flour. In the doorway of the cavernous warehouse, a group of men were filling a wagon with sacks even now.

An inn stood on the other side of the mill yard, far enough away to be spared the racket of its waterwheel and shouting laborers, but close enough not only to serve the custom of visiting merchants and teamsters, but beckon millworkers to its common room for a mug of ale or a hot meal before they headed home.

The front door was open. As Hyacinth crossed the threshold, she was greeted by the familiar scent of floorboards seasoned by decades of spilled drinks. At this hour there were no customers, but the place was bursting with activity, all of it originating from one source: A woman of about forty-five years was wiping off tables and clearing chairs from one side of the common room. A bucket of soapy water and a mop were waiting near the bar.

"Yes?" the woman asked.

"Do you have any rooms available?"

"Booked full and then some. King's wagons and twenty men arriving later today."

She did not stop wiping and clearing while she spoke. Hyacinth had rarely seen a skinny innkeeper, but she did not doubt how this woman stayed so lean.

"Do you have servants' quarters?" Hyacinth asked. "Because it looks like you are a little short-handed."

Finally the woman halted, hand poised over the mop handle, and studied Hyacinth straight on. "You have any experience?"

Hyacinth smiled. "A bit."

Without another word, she took the mop and set to work.

—o—

Ever since the incident at the campsite when she had been twelve, Hyacinth had always awakened early, never quite trusting the day to begin without bloodshed. And so she knew from the very first morning in Many Mills that its sunrise was one of its treasures. Immediately to the east, just across the river, the hillside rose well above the flood plain, leaving the village in shadow for nearly an hour after the sunbeams touched the hilltops to the west.

On this particular morning, Hyacinth rose even earlier than her custom and sat on the inn's raised porch so as to watch the process from the very start. The sky paled, rendering the ridgeline in silhouette. The heights emerged—a panoply of conifer, granite, and tiny waterfalls. The light grew and grew, and the world transformed from cloaked to revealed. No abruptness. No glare to keep her from witnessing every aspect.

She pulled her veneration plaque from her apron. She wet her fingertips with water from her flask, wrote her invocation with the moisture, and set the plaque down beside her.

A figure approached the inn carrying a sack. It was Hewer,

son of Mistress Summer, the innkeeper. His parents had named him well. Like his father, he was often working up in the hills with an axe, knocking down timber for one or another of the local sawmills. The work had left him with broad shoulders and sure-gripped hands. He was one of the youths who had admired Hyacinth at the fountain. Judging by the rich aroma of fresh bread coming from the sack, he had risen early to fetch his mother's order from the bakery in the main village.

"My ma doesn't have you scraping carrots or boiling eggs yet?" He grinned.

"Not today." She grinned back.

Mistress Summer had insisted Hyacinth take the morning off. The kingsmen had left, but a party of merchants was due to arrive on the morrow, and she declared it was important to rest. Not that Mistress Summer did. She and Hyacinth were alike in that way. They were alike in many ways, Hyacinth had found.

It was good to have the break. Every day and night for a week she had cleaned and served at table and washed bedding and fifty other tasks, while her uncle had served as barkeep and strongarm. Over those seven days, she had seen Mistress Summer's expression shift from weary to calm, her speech pattern from clipped to conversational. Last night when Hyacinth had lowered the foldaway pallet in the pantry to go to sleep, she had found a sprig of rosemary placed inside it to banish the vestiges of the previous tavern girl's sweat. That and the companionship of the pantry cat had made for a superior night of sleep.

"What was that you were doing?" Hewer asked. "With the plaque?"

"It's part of my ritual. I learned it during my time along the

Salt Coast. You use water to write about something unsatisfactory in the past. In a few moments it evaporates and you begin your new day freed of it."

"Does it work?"

She shrugged. "To the degree you let it."

She held up the plaque. The runes had almost evaporated. "Strictly speaking I'm supposed to use the language of the beachfolk, but I never learned the written form."

"I've never met anyone who has been as far as the Salt Coast."

"My uncle and I went farther than that, before we wound our way back."

"You must like the road."

"I wouldn't say that," she replied. "But there are good things about it."

"I want to hear more, if you have the time," he said.

"I do."

While he delivered the sack to the pantry, she fetched a trencher of bread and butter, an urn of muskberry jam, and a pot of fawnheather tea. They returned to the porch to watch the village awaken. And they talked. It was easy just to sit there, nibbling and sipping, alternately sharing more tales of her travels, but mostly just listening to Hewer's deep voice. He may not have seen much of the world, but he had seen a great many people pass through Many Mills and his mother's inn. He had the knack of describing them in such a way that she knew he knew them for what they were, and was neither fooled by the unworthy nor lacking in compassion for everyone else.

"Old Master Forktree, he always sits at the end of the corner bench. He met his first wife there, the one that had the bad miscarriage and died. I don't believe he has ever spoken of her once to the wife he has now. Been married to her fifty years. But he always sits there. She always lets him."

Eventually Hewer stood up to leave, off to help repair the rope bridge upstream. Hyacinth found herself wishing he could linger. She watched him as he walked away. Smiled at him when he turned to look. Then she rose and brushed the bread crumbs from her skirt, taking comfort in knowing they could pick up the conversation in the evening—a luxury she had not always enjoyed these past five years.

She immediately went to the scullery, where she washed the utensils and trencher. She stored the jar of jam back in the pantry and hung the wet dish towel from the line in the laundry courtyard. Checking the dried bedsheets that still hung there, the previous day having been so busy, she began folding them and placing them in a basket.

She was suddenly aware that someone was watching her from the doorway. It was Mistress Summer, who smiled at her warmly.

"I hope you understand how welcome you are. How well you fit in."

"Oh, yes," Hyacinth replied. "Very much."

As she said it, it sank in how true it was. What she was feeling now was more than the sense of being among good people or being appreciated for her contributions. She'd had that a number of times, from the journey on the barge when she was twelve, to the ocean crossings when she was fifteen, to the weeks at the scholar's sanctuary in the Cloudlands just last summer.

What she was feeling now was more than just a reaction to Mistress Summer's approval, or the appeal of Hewer's broad shoulders and kind eyes, or even being immersed once again in the routine of innkeeping. The last time she had felt this way was before her grandmother had died and her mother's health had turned bad, back when she could not have imagined ever living anywhere but in the village in which she had been born.

"What is it?" Mistress Summer asked. "You look so startled."

"I...need to ask you something."

—o—

She found her uncle walking back from the river, carrying a brace of fish he had caught.

"Why are you crying?" he asked.

She hesitated, toes grinding at the hard clay. She inhaled deeply.

"Uncle. I want to *stay.*"

"I know."

"You do?" She dabbed her eyelashes with her sleeves.

"It's what you've needed for some time now. This is a good place. Of course you should stay."

"But...you...?"

"We both know I have to go on." He held up the fish, turning them this way and that. The sunlight glittered on the scales. Bear's yearning, the locals called them. "I'll have a nice dinner tonight. Sleep in a good bed. And in the morning I'll be on my way. Whenever the hunters of the book manage to catch my scent again, they will have no reason to search here. You will be safe. As I promised."

"Will...will I ever see you again?"

"I am already counting the days," he replied.

Now the tears came in full. She collapsed against him, soaking the front of his shirt as she kept sobbing. For the rest of her life, whenever she smelled fresh-caught river fish, she would remember her uncle and all he meant to her.

—o—

Rowan did as he said. He left in the morning, having said his good-byes properly, having sworn Mistress Summer and her husband to look out for Hyacinth, and having handed over to his niece the small purse of gold he had been surreptitiously accumulating as her dowry over the past few years.

He left by the river road, heading the opposite way they had arrived. The burled terrain soon hid the village from view. The horse appreciated the chance to exercise after a week spent mostly in a paddock and Rowan did not rein in for a stop until well after the noon hour.

A meadow flocked with arched clover and lambsbell beckoned. Rowan hobbled his beast and set him out to graze. Rowan settled on a smooth log in the shade of a russetleaf and snacked on bread and some of the squeakcheese Mistress Summer had wrapped up for him just before he left. Licking his fingers and wiping them off, he fetched the book from his saddlebag.

He opened the volume to the usual spot, just before the uneven page that marked the present moment.

The leave-taking was bittersweet. Bitter because Rowan knew he was unlikely to ever have offspring of his own. His niece had been his daughter these five years. No one could replace her. The prospect of the loneliness to come wrapped iron weights around his ankles. Sweet because at last he was on his own again, freed from his worries about her wellbeing, knowing she was happy, and was likely to remain so.

A lavender-sweetened breeze fluffed the stallion's mane, urging him on. Rowan smiled.

Rowan lifted his nose from the book, and breathed in. Yes. Lavender. The perfumer he had heard tales of back in Many Mills must have fields somewhere up ahead. Not close—the aroma was still so subtle he would not have detected it unless trying to do so. The writer, whoever that magical entity might be, often noticed details he missed.

To read more, he would have to turn the page. If he did that, the page opposite would describe things that had not happened yet. Instead, he flipped back and began reading of the voyage he and Hyacinth had taken to the Vineyard Isle, and of the friendly seamstress whose company he had enjoyed during the crossing. It was one of his favorite chapters.

Long ago when he had first acquired the book, he had done as Hyacinth had done, and opened it to its end, only to find that section blank. He had conquered his curiosity before he encountered text, and his strength of will had not faltered since. He had never once read of future events. When Hyacinth had asked if she would be all right, he had not known it as a fact of history. He only knew that was the only right way for things to turn out, and had faith that it would somehow come to pass.

He always had liked a good story. It wouldn't do to spoil the ending.

THE BEHEADED QUEEN

Ten months had passed since my lord king had deigned to liberate me from my niche. Over the years, as his fury had dimmed, I had become little more to him than an ornament—akin perhaps to the portrait of his great-grandfather, the Reaver, that hung in his council chamber. In some ways the indifference was not unlike his treatment of me during our marriage.

The yeoman set me down on the pedestal beside the throne, where once my lesser chair had stood. He and a palace maid plucked the cobwebs from my eyebrows, brushed my hair, and dabbed oil of rose behind my ears.

"Regal Lady. By your leave, I will lift you from your tray," the yeoman said.

"Do as you will," I replied. My voice sounded peculiar to my ears. The enchantment did not permit me to speak when consigned to my niche. These were the first words I had uttered in three seasons.

He grasped me around the jaw and raised me. The maid removed the cloth that had lain beneath me. It was stained with a few drops of the blood that still brimmed at the end of my neck, fresh as the day the axeman had parted my head from my shoulders. The poor girl shuddered as she slipped the new linen into place.

They arranged me so that I faced the throne, not the gallery. This was the first clear sign that I was to be addressed by the king himself.

Pathren kept me in suspense nearly an hour—intentionally, I am sure. He entered alone, his men-at-arms left behind at their sentry stations at the great doors. Soon he loomed in front of me.

"Traitress," he greeted me.

"Murderer," I responded.

The last time I had called him anything other than "Father of My Sons," he had ordered me back to my niche and caused the drape to be closed, denying me the privilege of witnessing the doings of the court—the one diversion I had left to keep me from dwelling on my wretchedness. This time he did not react.

"It seems we are speaking," I said. "Why?"

"The crown prince is betrothed."

Had I still possessed a heart, it would have skipped a beat. "Bredden is to marry? When? To whom?"

"To Imileya, eldest daughter of the King of Fenmarch."

I had expected a different answer. Some unpleasant prospect, revealed to torment me. I had not smiled in years, but I was ready to now. "That is a superb match."

"It has advantages," admitted Pathren.

Then I saw the problem. "What does her father ask of you in return?"

"My watchtower at Goblin Pass."

"Are these terms you can bide by?"

He held his hand low, palm up in a curl, as he had in bygone times cupped my womanhood. A possessive pose. "The Reaver built that watchtower. It has been part of the realm for over a century." He sighed. "You are right. I cannot simply let Alvos have it."

"Yet the betrothal is a fact? You have agreed?"

"I have," he admitted. "We are committed to the courtship year."

"How can this be?"

"I have made peace with it in this way: I will give the watchtower to Bredden. He will pass it to Imileya as a wedding gift. For a number of years it will be manned by a garrison of her choosing—one from Fenmarch, if she likes. Upon her eventual death, title passes to her heir. Who will also be Bredden's heir. So the tower will ultimately be part of Sorregal again, and in the meantime, it will never actually belong to Alvos."

"I take it you will not put your seal upon the transfer until near the end of the courtship year?"

"Naturally."

So he had until next summer to reconsider. But if realized, these were unprecedented concessions on his part. He could not be the instigator of this scheme. "You are doing all this at Bredden's request," I said. It was not a question.

"I am."

"That was bold of him," I said. "How is it you did not tell him no?"

He shrugged. A simple gesture, and one more honest and unguarded than I had seen from him since we had been newlyweds.

"Bredden has always done as I have asked. Perhaps it is time to do as he asks, simply because he asks. He is the future of

Sorregal. It is his right to lay the foundation of his reign. I would rather see him do so now, while I am here to catch him if he stumbles. And if he should enjoy success, let it be while I am here to witness it."

Pathren was feeling his age. He had not been young when he took me to wife. He now had no trace of auburn left in his hair. It was all grey, as his beard had been for years.

"Nature will soon have its way with me. With Alvos as well. Our sons have less reason to hate one another. Diplomacy may succeed. If in the process Bredden wins himself a bride of quality, so much the better."

"Does she accept this marriage?"

"Now we come to the issue," said Pathren. "She has said yes, but she had little choice. Does she grasp what it should mean to be Bredden's wife? I would not care to see him played falsely."

As he gazed at me, a glimmer of the old rage flickered.

I said nothing. Any comment would only have sent him into a litany of my crimes. That was a speech I had heard too many times.

"I have made a pact with Bredden," he went on. "Father to son. King to crown prince. During this coming year, while Imileya dwells among us here in Sorregal, things must go well. If they do, the wedding will be held. If they do not, the betrothal shall be dissolved. And I keep my watchtower."

"How would you determine if it has 'gone well?'"

"In sundry ways, but only one that need involve you. I must be satisfied of Imileya's nature. Will she be loyal to Bredden, or an agent of Fenmarch? Will she be a source of harmony in my castle, or a seed of dissension? You are to judge."

I could barely credit what I had heard. "I?"

"You. It cannot be left to Bredden. If the sight and scent of Imileya makes him keen to get between her legs, he will be blinded to any flaws she has. I need a woman's perspective. I would not trust the assessments of the ladies of my court. They all have their own schemes in play. You are the mother of the Heir. You will want what is genuinely best for him."

"That could not be more true."

"Then we have an accord. You will leave in the morning with the entourage I am sending to fetch Imileya from Fenmarch. You will observe the princess closely from the moment you meet her. She may reveal herself in her homeland and on the journey in ways that she will not once she is ensconced within these walls, among folk entirely alien to her."

"A boon," I asked. "Fetch Bredden here. Let me see him before I go."

He chuckled. "He is already waiting."

He yanked the pull-cord. The bell of summoning resounded beyond the great doors.

Pathren rotated my tray so that I faced the supplicant's dais. Through the archway strode a young, strapping man I barely recognized. I had not seen Bredden since he had left for the wars in the south, to learn first-hand the leading of the kingdom's warriors, and to prove himself in their eyes.

Slight scars ran across his chin and right cheek—not enough to mar his handsomeness, but enough to show he had not shirked from danger on the battlefield. His armor rode smartly on his broad frame. His eyes were alert and evaluating. Yet I sensed all was not well. He was changed. Hardened. He stopped before me and gave a short bow, not deep, but precisely proper for a crown prince addressing his mother. Too proper for my liking.

"Madam, it is good to see you."

"You are a boy no longer," I murmured. Tears welled in the corners of my eyes. They did not drip down my cheeks, but it was not for lack of emotion on my part. In my current state I neither drank nor ate. The potions the demon swabbed into my mouth each month sustained me, but they did not grant me the moistness needed to weep.

"No. I am not. Not for some time."

"Are you of a mind to marry?"

"I am."

"Then we will speak of it."

I paused.

He understood at once. "Sir?" he said, turning to Pathren. "Might I hear my mother's counsel in private?"

Pathren canted an eyebrow at us, but he made no protest. Soon Bredden and I had the throne room to ourselves.

"I have heard the reports of your doings," I told my son. "You have accounted well for yourself. No one questions your fitness to lead the realm when your time comes. Even your father sees it."

"I found the strength you spoke of," he said. He did not say it triumphantly. Now that we were alone the anguish in him was vivid.

"What is it?" I asked gently.

"Such things I have seen. Such actions I have had to take. With a word I change the course of men's lives, or end those lives. I scarce know myself any longer."

"My precious boy," I murmured. "You must not despair. You have come far."

"But in what direction?" he asked.

I had never seen him so troubled. I could not know all that fueled it. When he had been young, nothing that went on inside him was opaque to me. Now he was encased within the armor of a king-to-be, and I could not know all he was. The one thing I could know with certainty is that it was no whim that had caused him to pursue a marriage at this time.

"You look to a wife to serve as your gauge." I smiled. "I gave birth to no fool."

He leaned close, undaunted by the eldritch aroma that my flesh gave off. "She must be the right one, Mother. I do not fear the battlefield. I fear only what I may be, with the wrong voice in my ear at night."

"What do you know of Imileya, to make your overture to her?"

"I have heard tales enough to give me hope. But in the end, I know no more than anyone in Sorregal. Is she right for me? If anyone can judge this, it is you, Mother."

"I will do all I can," I said. "And Bredden?"

"Yes, Mother?"

"Blessings upon you, to give me this task."

"Blessing are already upon me," he answered, "or you would not be here to give the task to." He kissed my forehead.

Ten years I had suffered. Now I knew there was meaning to my survival.

—o—

In the morning the cortege gathered in the main courtyard. A miniature palanquin had been created for me. It required only two bearers given the slight weight I represented, even taking into account the thick brass accouterments and the heft of the canopy. The bearers were robust plainsmen; they would easily be able to keep up. The knights were riding their battle mounts, and while those beasts might handle the burden of a man in chain mail with admirable fortitude, they could not cover long distances day after day faster than men could walk those same leagues.

Aside from me and my bearers, the party consisted of ten noblemen and twice that number of men-at-arms, along with a number of squires and grooms, a cook, and a cook's boy. And one other person. She came out of the castle last, wearing a spotless riding dress of cream silk with spun-gold embroidery. The tiara in her hair sparkled when she emerged from the shadow of the building.

I had barely seen my eldest daughter since the days when I had possessed arms and a lap to nestle her within. Bredden had visited me whenever Pathren would permit it. Clessa had never come of her own accord. We had not been in each other's immediate presence since an occasion when she had disobeyed her governess, and had been brought to my niche as a lesson in what could happen to a royal female who misbehaved. She had run screaming from the chamber.

She paused at my palanquin. She eyed me coldly. A slight tremor betrayed that she yearned to flee the sight of me again.

"Daughter," I said. "You are a striking young woman."

"Lovely princesses make the best hostages," she quipped, and stalked away to her horse.

—o—

Clessa made a point to avoid me in the early part of our

travels. I did not contend with her over it. She was already being forced to spend a year in a foreign land as surety for Imileya—one king's daughter for another. I would only have her bide with me if it were her own will.

I did not lack for distraction. The countryside was a marvel to me. For years all I had seen was the audience chamber and on occasion, when Pathren wanted to display me to the populace, I had been suspended in a cage from the parapet overlooking the square. No matter how many times I had soared over the land in my dreams, the confinement had wreaked its dulling effect. I had forgotten the scratchiness of the scent of threshed hay, the lusty attitude in the twitter of birdsong. Days brightened of nature's accord, and not because palace servants lit lamps.

We reached the mountains on the fifth day. For the first time I could see for myself what was meant by the palisades. Not just mountain slopes, but cliffs and treacherous banks of talus shielded our kingdom—save for Goblin Pass, where the glaciers of the high slopes sent their meltwater down, carving into the weak spot in the range, feeding the River of Alders. Even from the valley I could see the saddle of the divide, the one place where no snow-laden peaks blocked our path.

"Were you ever as far as this, when you were alive?" The speaker's pitch was girlish, but the delivery assertively mature.

The nose of Clessa's mount advanced into my field of view— but only far enough to bring Clessa herself straight to the left of my perch. Since my ability to swivel my head was minor, I was left unable to regard her. Which she well knew.

"I am still alive," I said. "Your father's bonded demon makes sure of that."

"Do you not wish to be dead?"

"I have wished it and I have wished it," I replied. "But no one has been willing to incur His Royal Majesty's wrath and give me my release. Will *you* do it?"

"No."

"Then I will die when Pathren dies, and his demon returns to its realm. In the meantime I linger, the better to demonstrate the power of the king."

"I thought it was to demonstrate the depth of your offense."

Many felt as she did, but it hurt more to hear it from my own offspring. "I committed no wrong. Or none, that is, save that I put my trust in a lady-in-waiting who did not deserve it."

She gasped. "No wrong? You were an adulteress."

"And the king was an adulterer. With a hundred women. Two hundred."

"That is different. It was of no consequence to him. What you did was hateful."

"On the contrary. I did not hate your father. Not then. Though I had come to see him for the sort of man he was."

"And what sort was that?"

"Need I tell you?"

She hesitated.

"He is the kind a demon would serve," I pointed out. "And they are not beings who serve a man whose nature is sweet."

"But he was the king. You had a duty," she said.

"Yes. I did. And I was conscious of it. Spite would never have been enough to lead me down my path. I did as I did because of my feelings for Faeyn, and of his for me. Those feelings were the opposite of hate."

"Do not speak his name. It is forbidden."

"Faeyn, Faeyn, Faeyn," I said, wishing I could shout, but to do that required lungs I did not have. "And I lay with him *many* times."

"You are the harlot everyone says you are!"

"You decided that long ago, I think. If it is guilt you want, you will not get it from me. If you had ever been in love, you might have some concept of why I acted as I did."

"I have been in love," she objected.

"Oh?"

I waited. She tightened in the saddle enough that her mount quickened its pace. Before she restored her position I glimpsed the blush in her cheeks.

"Not the kind of love to make me... lose my head," she admitted.

"Well put."

—o—

The last morning of our ascent, the proximity to the snowline rendered the air brisk. I, who had been tucked away so long, appreciated the novelty of my skin prickling and was disappointed that I had no breath to make little clouds in front of my face. But Clessa whined, as only a princess raised in comfort can whine. For the sake of my ears, I resolved that our quarters in the watchtower would be separated by at least one thick stone wall.

At the top of the pass, we announced our arrival with a trumpet blast and a waving of the king's standard. Men of the local garrison responded in kind. To my surprise, we did not head for the redoubt at the base of the promontory on which the keep stood, though its portcullis was lifted as we drew near. Instead the retinue gathered in formation to face an encampment that lay several hundred paces down the road that led to Fenmarch.

"Fortune be with you, Your Majesty," said Lord Ullank, the Earl of Rowanwood, the highest ranking of our escorts.

"You go no farther?" I asked.

"Terms of the truce, these past sixteen years. No warrior of Sorregal may go beyond this point. No warrior of Fenmarch may come closer than a bowshot from the northern wall." He gestured at the archers along the battlements of the watchtower.

It seemed there would be no night of peace and solitude for me, nor any big stone hearth to melt the icicle that had apparently formed in Clessa's rectum. I wondered if Pathren had told them to leave me unaware that the exchange would happen at the instant of our arrival, or if they had kept the secret out of personal disrespect.

Clessa whimpered, having grasped that the moment had come when she was to be abandoned into the keeping of strangers, to become a hostage in truth.

"Fortune be with you all," I called to the cortege. Ullank gestured to my bearers and I and my palanquin were carried into the no man's land. I heard the erratic clip-clop of horse hoofs as Clessa followed. She kept slowing down, then having to catch up.

The strangers ahead began breaking down their tents and stowing gear in panniers and in mule packs. The group was similar in size and composition to our own. From the look of the trampled ground they had been on site about two days.

Once we were twice bowshot distance from the fortifications, one of the Fenmarchers mounted his horse and advanced toward us at a rate that perfectly matched our approach, as ritual called for. The rider's helm was decorated with a single, elegant plume of rank.

"Pus and gore," Clessa muttered. "They've sent a *boy*."

"Hush," I said.

He was no boy. He was tall and well-knit. His beard was full. As he reined up and dismounted, his movements exuded grace.

He removed his helmet and placed it under an arm. "Your Majesty, Queen Daena. Your Highness, Princess Clessa," he said, bowing to each of us in turn. "I bring you greetings from Alvos the Fourth, King of Fenmarch."

"Well met," I answered. "And you are...?"

"I am Norl of Heronpool."

"You are more than that, I think."

"I am the viscount of Heronpool, if it please Your Majesty."

Clessa snorted.

"Forgive my daughter's manners," I said. "She had no mother to teach her better, these past ten years. You are Madrak's heir?"

"I am."

"Then you are one-and-twenty. It does you credit you do not flaunt a title you've so newly acquired."

"You are kind, Ma'am."

"Clessa," I said. "Your father's men cut down Madrak, Viscount of Heronpool, at the Battle of Eagles. This young man was—what, six years old at the time?"

"Not quite, ma'am."

"Five, then. I would not antagonize him, girl. He might take that axe from his saddle and trim your toenails."

He smiled.

Clessa hiccupped.

"It seems we are in your charge now," I told Heronpool. "Lead on. How many days shall we be? I am anxious to meet my future daughter-in-law."

Away went the cheeriness I had managed to engender. "Six days," he said pensively. "Six days."

—o—

The journey continued as soon as our new escorts finished loading their gear. It was obvious the Fenmarchers had no desire to spend another night in the vicinity of the watchtower.

Several hours later, we came to a place where the land dropped away. Heronpool ordered everyone into a single file, riders on foot leading their mounts. We proceeded along a path that was often so narrow the warhorses barely squeezed along. Here and there retaining walls and bridges of stout rope and planks proved this was an official route, maintained by Alvos's roadsmen, but most sections of it had been etched into the mountainside by no method more elaborate than the action of foot, hoof, and boot over a period of centuries.

From time to time I caught a glimpse of trailside brush, a rock outcropping, or a wind-twisted canyon juniper, but for the most part I saw little. The steepness of the terrain kept the palanquin canted at an angle, and so just before heading down, my servants had fastened padding tight around me to keep me from rolling off. This left me in a bowl that obscured much of my view. To make matters worse, on the second switchback I toppled onto one ear.

I did not call out. It was difficult enough to be so dependent on others for simple locomotion. I refused to have to beg for aid.

The person who came to my rescue was none other than Heronpool. He had stationed himself at a widening of the trail in order to inspect his company as it passed by. When he saw what had become of me, he halted my palanquin and set me upright.

"Thank you," I said.

"You are welcome," he answered. From that point on, wherever the trail's width permitted it, he walked beside the palanquin.

In the midst of the next section of trail, the stench of horse dung wafted strongly over us. Freed of the weight of their riders, it seemed many animals had been inspired to void their bowels, doing so at the very part of the journey when we were least able to avoid the fumes. Heronpool leaned down at trailside and plucked a flower. He lay the bloom next to my cheek, where its scent predominated.

I smiled as I took in the aroma. It was musky, very much like bell lily, a favorite of mine. "What do you call this?"

"Snow lily," he replied. "It grows only in these heights."

Eventually the grade was interrupted by a broad ledge. Here the company halted so that the knights could rest, and the grooms give the horses and mules a few mouthfuls of feed and some water.

My bearers set me down. To their credit, they chose a spot as far from the brink as they could. But as usual, they gave no thought to my angle of view.

Heronpool was not so unsolicitous. "The vantage here is like nothing else in the kingdom," he said. "Do you wish to see?"

"Very much," I replied.

He cradled me and my seep-cloth in his hands and carried me to an outlook. Finally I could properly gaze at the vista. He was correct. It was magnificent. A gorge of timbered slopes, granite faces, and waterfalls gave way to a plain of pastures, tilled fields, villages, and of course, some of the wetlands for which Fenmarch was named. Mists were burning off in the lowest places, revealing dripping green foliage and gleaming lakes.

"You are kind to me, Count Heronpool. You freely do what my own subjects would not, even should I ask."

"You are treated cruelly," he replied. "Should I echo it? I would think less of myself if I did."

I liked him. He was a confident young buck, but in him, poise had led to forthrightness rather than arrogance.

"Tell me, sir. Do you think me a criminal?"

He hesitated.

"Please, speak you mind. I take no offense. I have no tender parts left."

"Were you guilty?" he asked.

"I cuckolded the king, if that's what you mean."

"Then yes, you are a criminal."

"But not deserving of cruelty?"

"No one deserves that. A king's laws and a king's will must be obeyed, but mercy is the mark of a true sovereign. Surely, in your case, a simple execution would have sufficed."

"Would Alvos have been merciful?"

"He is a stern king, but he is just."

"It seems I married the wrong prince," I said. "Not that I could have done otherwise. A woman of my rank rarely gets to choose her bridegroom."

He was silent.

"Is aught wrong, Count Heronpool?"

"These are somber matters we speak of, Ma'am. Let us enjoy

the view. We must be on our way again soon, if we are to reach the best place to camp for the night."

He was right. Enjoy the view I did, along with the lingering essence of snow lily.

—o—

The following day brought us into heavy stands of timber. Here Heronpool again demonstrated his quality.

Clessa was riding just ahead of my palanquin. I do not know what signal of danger alerted Heronpool. Perhaps he heard a creak as a bowstring tightened, perhaps he caught a glimpse of an enemy rising from a place of concealment. Whatever it was, he suddenly leaped from his mount, yanked Clessa out of her saddle, and threw her to the ground, covering her with his own armored form.

Arrows sang through the air. One whisked through the space I had just occupied, missing me only because my bearers had plunged into defensive squats.

Things happened very quickly after that, so quickly I could hardly follow it all. Heronpool sprang to his feet, barking directives. I think he said, "Archers, 'ware the branches. The rest, to your tandems."

His men understood their roles well. Most, I believe, were in motion even before he spoke. His archers fired into the trees. I heard grunts of pain and heavy impacts; they had hit at least two targets. Other knights charged around nearby trees, any with boles large enough to conceal ambushers. They moved in pairs, the first man with shield set to deflect arrows or blades, the second following with a weapon out, ready to seize the offensive.

The closest exchange happened right where I could witness it all transpire. A tandem met a brigand as he charged from a camouflaged hollow.

The brigand was a large, formidable man. He kicked so hard he knocked the shield man over. His prowess was such that when the second man skewered him with a pike thrust, he still managed to swing his axe and crush the pike wielder's ribcage. Only then did he fall.

The pikeman swayed. His knees buckled as his partner reached him and helped him to the ground.

With that, the battle ended, save for one fleeing man being noisily cut down in a patch of bracken well away from the trail. There had been no more than half a dozen ambushers. They had come to achieve their goal with stealth and surprise, not force of arms.

A few paces from me Clessa sat up, eyes narrowing as she surveyed the dirt on her dress. Muttering, she rubbed the hip she had landed upon when Heronpool had tugged her from the saddle.

Heronpool returned, having established that the threat was dealt with, and having ordered further scouting of the vicinity.

"You read the situation well," I told him. "If I am not mistaken those first arrows were aimed at Clessa."

My daughter's sputters ceased. Her eyes widened. As I had suspected, she had not grasped the nature of what had just happened, and how fortunate she was to be alive.

"We were too strong a party for robbers to trifle with," Heronpool confirmed. "So they had to be assassins, sent to kill the royal hostage and spoil the peacemaking."

"Thank the viscount, Clessa."

Her hands were trembling. She pressed her bosom, as if needing to quiet her heart before she could utter a word. "Th-thank you, Count Heronpool."

"I am charged with your safety. I simply did my duty. You can thank me by agreeing to wear armor until we clear the forest."

"As you wish," she said. I was pleased to hear what I accepted as genuine humility in her tone.

"I see you are anxious to go to your man over there," I said. "Please do not tarry on our account. I fear he is not long for this world."

I had not even finished my statement before Heronpool knelt where his fallen comrade lay at the base of a piedmont cedar. The loam beneath the latter's torso was dark. Crimson froth leaked from his mouth as he labored to draw breath.

Heronpool clasped the pikeman's hand, providing something to squeeze during the spasms of pain. "I will tell all of your valor."

The dying man looked at Heronpool imploringly, but his attempt to speak only produced a gurgling cough. Heronpool understood despite the lack of words.

"Your widow and son need not fear. If need be I will take them into my own castle until their situation is resolved. Her name is Mantha. The boy is Vristin. I swear I will look after their welfare."

The deep creases in the pikeman's brow eased. He closed his eyes. His chest still rose and fell, but weakly. It would be not long now. Heronpool remained, keeping the vigil.

"Clessa," I said.

"M-mother?"

"Our destination is too far off to take the body with us. The rites must be held here. Begin gathering deadfall branches for the pyre. Carry the wood personally. Pile it where they recommend. Do you understand?"

"I do, Mother."

She did as I asked. It seemed that even with this child, I might still do some good.

—o—

When we reached the capital of Fenmarch, the townsfolk gawked and exclaimed during our procession through the streets. Surely they had been told the visiting queen would consist of a head on a cushioned platform, but apparently it had not struck them as something they might confirm for themselves.

Twice, rotten fruit was flung at me and at Clessa. Then excrement. The barrages came from deep within the crowds and did not strike, save for specks of dung on the livery of my forward bearer. Each time, the city constables quickly clubbed anyone who might have been the offenders, before the misbehavior was imitated at a mob level. Heronpool and all his men rode with weapons bared.

I feared their precautions would not be enough. These people had long thought of Sorregal as Fenmarch's greatest enemy. Some, like the assassins in the forest, would never accept the prospect of an alliance. But we passed over the drawbridge of Alvos's castle before any lasting harm was done.

The palace staff was waiting in the courtyard. The chamberlain approached me and bowed. "Your chambers have been made ready, Your Majesty. When you and the princess have refreshed yourselves, the royal family beckons you to the queen's parlor."

It suited me that we were to be met intimately and out of public view, in the traditional manner. In the same spirit of courtesy, I made sure we did not keep our hosts waiting overlong, though this required haranguing Clessa to finish her bath and primping with what must, to her, have been unprecedented alacrity.

"Your hair is fine just like that," I told her as she checked her reflection yet again.

She frowned as she approached me. "I really have to carry you myself?"

"It is the only proper way," I said firmly. "And do have a care not to trip. I should not wish to meet Queen Vamia by rolling across her parlor carpet and ending up under her skirts."

Clessa was a robust girl and managed the weight quite easily once she put her mind to it. The chamberlain announced us and we issued smoothly into a sumptuously appointed room. I immediately knew Vamia to be one of those women who compensates for personal lack of beauty by surrounding herself with loveliness. The tapestries and furnishings were of the highest order, and the attire of everyone in the room, even the servants, was resplendent.

The whole ruling clan was there, from Alvos and Vamia to all three princes and their wives to Imileya and her sisters to the white-haired, blind, and quite toothless queen mother. Clessa must not have expected to be outnumbered so dramatically; her hands shook as she set me down. I briefly wobbled on the pedestal that had been provided for me in the center of the room.

Imileya, fortune be praised, had inherited none of the prunish features of her mother—luck of which her sisters could not boast. I suspected Bredden would have preferred a wife with more bosom, but all in all it did not appear he would have cause to rue what he would find in his bed come the wedding night.

I was struck, however, by what an unanimated expression she wore. She might have been made of wax. I cannot say that everyone in the group smiled as we came into the room, but all seemed to be making the attempt, save her.

Clessa curtsied. The others responded, and greetings and introductions went all round.

"I am told of bloodshed in the mountains," Alvos said. "And a lack of manners from some of the common folk in the streets today. I offer you my apologies."

"No need. Thanks to your protective measures, we are here and unruffled. May I commend in particular your choice of Count Heronpool as chief escort?"

"He is the most loyal man I have," the king said. "A pity he is so low-ranking a peer."

I had thought the compliment a fine way to brighten the conversation, but in its wake the king seemed if anything more taciturn. I would recall this later, though at that moment I credited his subsequent silence to his intrinsic nature.

The crown prince, he who was in line to become Alvos the Fifth, was more demonstrative. When he said it was the privilege of Fenmarch to keep Clessa as their guest for the year, he sounded so sincere Clessa actually smiled.

More pleasantries ensued. Whether we had an audience or not, I knew this would be the way of it, for to speak of anything controversial or unresolved at this point would be an unforgivable breach of protocol. Finally the time came for Clessa and me to return to our guest quarters, and the family to their suites, in order to prepare for supper.

"Imileya," said her mother, "you have not given Queen Daena your kisses."

Imileya blanched. It was the first real reaction I had seen from her.

Vamia frowned. Alvos opened his mouth for what I am sure would be a command for Imileya to obey her mother's directive.

"I am less kissable than I once was," I interjected. "If it please you, Clessa will be my proxy."

Vamia and Alvos looked at one another, and shrugged.

Imileya rose from her divan, jittery with relief. She kissed my daughter on each cheek, and Clessa responded in kind.

Everyone present appeared satisfied that etiquette had been observed. Once Imileya was certain no further ordeal was involved, she allowed herself to look straight at me. She blushed.

"Do not fret," I said. "We have plenty of time to get to know one another."

At this, she went pale again.

—o—

The next evening a great banquet was held in celebration of the betrothal. Though I of course could not partake of the food, I was given the seat of honor at the foot of the high table, directly opposite Alvos and Vamia. Imileya was seated at the king's right. The arrangement gave me a fine opportunity to observe my daughter-in-law to be; moreover, I could do so from a distance where she would not overly conscious of the scrutiny.

Her role for the next few hours was to graciously accept the best wishes of the peers of the realm who had gathered for this last formal opportunity to convey their respects before she was trundled off to Sorregal. She handled the obligation with aplomb. I was encouraged to see it, for it showed she might do equally well in years to come at state functions as Bredden's queen.

But in between the speeches and the presentation of gifts, when allowed to sit and partake of her repast, she was overly quiet. Almost absent. She was only at ease when she could slip into responses of the sort any princess rehearses throughout her upbringing.

And then I caught a glimpse of the true Imileya.

She tried to be furtive, but I saw her attention drift to her right, across the table and slightly toward my end. Her glance paused on a young noble seated there.

It was Norl, Viscount of Heronpool.

Aside from Clessa, he was the one person present with whom I was acquainted to any degree, and so I had watched him, growing ever more curious why he stared so much at his plate. It certainly would not have been his interest in the food, for he ate half-heartedly and in small quantity. Now he tilted his head up and it happened that his and Imileya's gazes met.

For a moment—no more the time it took the king to lift his goblet from table to mouth—Imileya looked at Heronpool, and he looked at her.

Suddenly, I was twelve years in the past. Suddenly, I was no bodiless head. I had a heart to feel, hands with which to caress, a womanhood ready to be filled. I was gazing into the eyes of Faeyn, back in those heady days when we had recently become lovers. My nostrils widened. Air flowed into my chest. My heart began to thump. A warmth and a dampness claimed me down low, abrupt and intense—a reaction so beyond my ability to contain that it embarrassed me.

That was how it had been with me. Now, here, at this moment, that was how it was with Imileya. She shone with it. Here was a person wholly unlike the numbed, affectless princess I had seen until now.

I knew then what I had to do.

—o—

Four days after my arrival, the return cortege assembled in the courtyard below the main keep. Alvos stood on a balcony, observing the leavetaking where he could pretend to be stoic. Heronpool had been right to call his king stern, but I did not believe Alvos found it easy to let his child go. I suspected tears had been shed earlier, in private.

Clessa hovered near, chewing her lower lip while the saddles were cinched and final tallies of supplies counted off.

"Have you come to say good-by, child?" I asked.

She jumped at the sound of my voice. "What if all goes awry?" She was trembling. "What if I am left a prisoner here forever?"

"Attend to the things you can influence," I advised. "Make friends here, and no matter what happens in Sorregal, you may thrive."

She pondered this. "Mother?"

"Yes?"

"If I do return, I would like to talk with you more often."

"I would like that," I said.

Across the courtyard the leader of the cortege put in his first appearance. It was none other than Heronpool. All at once, Imileya's attention shifted from the balcony to the level of our company. She tried her best not to stare straight at the viscount, but I was not fooled.

—o—

We set out across the lowlands of Fenmarch. Day by day, the mountains rose higher across our horizon. I found Heronpool difficult to engage in conversation. He had been given to serious moods the whole time I had known him, but now he was downright solemn.

Imileya contrived at least once a day to ride beside him. He did not, as far as I could tell, attempt to seek her out in kind. They were always too far to allow me to eavesdrop, but I noted that they did not smile. They did not gesture at this and that, as would two people talking about the view or recounting anecdotes meant to entertain. On the afternoon we reached the foothills, Imileya stiffened at whatever he said to her, and Heronpool parted from her with abruptness, ostensibly to tell a man to fasten a pack mule's load better.

Imileya's posture changed. She was a capable horsewoman, and typically rode with spine straight and hands easy on the reins. But from that point on she sagged, and her mare took its cues from the animal ahead of it.

—o—

We passed through the forest where the assassins had

attacked our party, and in due course we reached the steep grade. The sun had only just hidden itself behind a peak to the west, but Heronpool declared we would set up camp at the base of the incline, to leave us fresh for the climb. I judged we would negotiate the highest switchback by noon the next day. After that the final leg to the watchtower would be only a matter of hours.

The men occupied themselves setting up cookfires, stowing gear, and seeing to the horses and mules. Imileya kept stealing glances at Heronpool. The viscount pretended to be preoccupied with his responsibilities.

As usual, the tent I shared with the princess was the first to be set up. I told my bearers to place me inside at once. "Come, girl," I told Imileya. "We must talk."

When we were settled, I on my high cushioned stool and Imileya on one of normal height, so that we faced one another at the same eye level, I told my bearers to leave, and to be sure no one was lurking within hearing range.

Imileya fidgeted. "What is it, ma'am? Is aught wrong?"

"Tonight is your last night in the territory of Fenmarch. We will reach the watchtower tomorrow well before sunset."

"I have been told as much," she said.

"Then tonight is your last chance to lie with Heronpool."

Her stool rocked back, and she nearly tumbled before she restored her balance. "What are you on about? Do you seek to trap me?"

"It is no trap. If you wish it, I would allow you to stow me in that chest over there, tucked among your scarves and belts, whilst you and Heronpool seize your moment. If I am ever asked, I will swear I attended you throughout the night, and no man visited you."

"You are a madwoman."

"Granted," I said. "My head was chopped off. My lover was tortured and killed in front of my eyes. For ten years I have been loathed, even by some of my children. Would your priorities not change, had you gone through all that? I tell you the offer is real. Do you not wish to lie with Heronpool? Are you not in love with him? Have you not already consummated your affection in seasons past?"

She quailed. "Am I so transparent?"

"To me? Yes. You must learn to be more circumspect. Heronpool has the knack well enough. I will coach you. A queen must excel in hiding secrets."

"You speak as if you would let me become queen, given what you know."

"I will," I said. "I believe you are right for my son."

"How can that be?" she said, her tone growing miserable. "For I would take your offer. I would lie with Heronpool. I would ravish him all this night. But he will not be part of it. Not now I am betrothed to another man."

"Oh, my dear girl," I said. "I am so sorry."

She hiccupped. Her voice grew hoarse. "I would have run away with him a month ago, if he had been willing."

"You need not explain," I said. "Duty. Honor."

Tears began to pour down her cheeks. "Yes."

"In him, those principles trump passion. The important thing is that in you, they do not. You would have lain with him." I gave her as tender a smile of approval as I had ever summoned for anyone other than Bredden. "You have a fire in you. You failed to suppress it even when displaying it put your very life at risk. My son needs a companion with such fire."

"But surely, he would be angry with me, if he knew."

"I do not say you should tell him. I do say that if you were a woman of ice, you would be no good to him. His spirit would dwindle with such a mate as that."

"But I do not burn for *him*."

"No. Not yet."

"How can I ever?"

"Because you must?" I asked.

She uttered a small squeak.

In the gentlest voice I could manage, I said, "Tell me what you love most about Heronpool."

When she let the question truly infiltrate her consciousness, she smiled. "His compassion. His—oh, it is many things. He is *inspiring*."

"And so he is," I said. "Tell me, do you think he is the only man in the world of such character?"

She blinked.

"Tonight, it seems, will be a lonely one," I told her in fervent sympathy. "Tomorrow will be bitter. Your heart will break when your beloved turns and rides the other way. But in a year, my daughter? In a year, there will be a wedding. I believe it will be a happy occasion for all concerned. Do you think me mad to say so?"

She stared at me full on, her cheeks and lashes wet, her hands tightly clasped in her lap. I could have been looking in a mirror, cast back to the point when I was a bride-to-be, about to meet my betrothed. But my destiny had thrust me into the arms of Pathren. She was intended for Bredden. That was an entirely different thing.

"You are indeed a madwoman," Imileya murmured. "But you are growing on me."

THE ETHERINE ROAD

"She's drunk again," the guard said as he unlocked the door to the witch's aerie.

Fox heard singing. Off-key. Hoarse. Simultaneously boisterous and bitter.

He found the witch floating just under the rafters at the limit of her tether, her short hair waving about her head like filaments of anemone.

"Don't mind me," she called down. "I'm just enjoying the view."

There was no view other than through the arrow slits—apertures that were all angled downward, the better to permit archers to release their missiles at those who might attack the castle's main gates. Housing his sister in quarters with true windows was not a risk the king was willing to take.

"You would think they'd let you look up," he commented. "All things considered."

"No matter," she hiccupped. "After all, I'm made to look

down."

The witch pushed off a cornice and drifted nearer, squinting.

"You *are* Sir Foxtread, are you not?"

"Indeed I am, Your Highness."

"You don't look the same."

"I try never to look the same twice. I'm sure you'll appreciate the reasoning."

"Mmm. Yes. I liked the beard, though." She raised her goblet to her mouth and inverted it. One last drop fell on her tongue. "I suppose if you're here, I can't have a refill."

"I'm afraid not. Duty calls. You must sober up."

"What's the fun in that?" she asked.

"None at all," he admitted.

He hooked one of his feet beneath the counterweight and pulled her down to her chair. She tried to strap herself in, but her fingers were no more deft than a bowl of noodles. He took over. A heavy aroma of pomegranate brandy wafted over him when she exhaled.

She studied him while he tightened the buckles. It was a sort of scrutiny Fox was no longer used to. Most people were daunted by the prospect of examining him within range of his knife.

She ran a finger along the tattoos lining the inside of his forearm, the account of which masters he had studied with, and in which assassin's arts he had earned his marque.

"You're so much smaller than the others. How did you get to be so deadly?"

"I move quietly. It's why they call me Foxtread."

"That's how it will be tonight?"

"Yes. Either I will be stealthy, or I will not live to see the dawn."

"Must we do this?" she asked.

"The prey we hunt is an evil man."

She let go of his arm. She turned her gaze away. "As evil as the king?"

Fox stood. "That's quite a question. All I can tell you is, it's not our task to kill the king."

"I am weary of deaths," she murmured. "Evil men or not."

Fox wanted to fold her hands in his, tell her she need have no part in the mission. But he couldn't offer her that. He couldn't even offer her a drink.

"You must help me fulfill this task, Your Highness. You know that."

She sagged. Or would have sagged, had she been any other sort of woman. Heaviness was not a thing she could manifest. Her form still tugged at the straps, wanting to return to the ceiling. Her bosom still rode as high as a maiden's. She was old enough now she should have had a slackness to her features, but no flesh had settled along her jawline.

"As you say, Sir Foxtread. Tonight we fly."

"The maidservants will be here soon to get you ready," he said. "I will see you at nightfall at the platform."

—o—

Fox arrived at the towertop while the sky to the west was still buttery. He watched dusk settle over the kingdom. There was no better place to do that than here.

Mount Smoke faded into the dimness to the southeast. Bats emerged from their roosts in the old keep across the river. In the streets below, tavernkeepers lit their lintel lamps.

The king's chamberlain led the witch's entourage. The witch herself emerged from the stairwell between two hefty guards, the counterweights dangling from her belt making it possible for her to actually walk on her feet. A pair of servant girls brought up the rear.

The witch had been sewn into her flight harness. The amulet had been padlocked in place at her sternum. Newly activated, it gave off pulses of midnight blue light. It was just enough illumination that Fox could see the lines in the witch's forehead, the evidence of her hangover.

The chamberlain gave a down-the-nose glance at Fox. Such an odious man. Fox hoped one day to throttle his birdlike neck, one day when a better regime was in power.

At the pedestal at the center of the platform, the chamberlain set his hand on the lodestone and recited the incantation. The sphere moaned to life.

The chamberlain gestured peremptorily at the witch. With a weary sigh, she set her hand to her amulet and uttered, "The King's Welcome."

The amulet began trying to tug her forward. Once the guards removed the weights on her belt and released their grip on her arms, she floated over to the pedestal. Her velocity slowed as she drew near, so that when the amulet and the lodestone finally touched, the contact was as soft as a kiss.

Now that the witch was anchored in place by the magic, the servant girls rolled up her cape. Her tunic's design left much of her back bare. Pale skin was revealed to the moonlight. One of the girls took talc from a sack and spread it over the area.

Fox unlaced his vest, exposing the front of his torso. The other girl spread talc upon him.

The chamberlain handed him the vial of potion. The elixir trickled down his throat slow as honey and with none of the sweetness. Fox struggled not to gag.

The chamberlain snickered.

When the dose had done its work, Fox pressed himself against the witch's back. He waved away the servant girls as they started to buckle the straps that would fasten tunic to vest. He would have to free himself in a few hours. Best that he confirmed now that the bonds were all within his reach.

Her back was cold against him. Eldritch cold. It went from that to numb as the enchantment blended into him. The tug of the earth faded. Unlike the two previous times he had endured it, the transition did not make him queasy. He settled immediately into the peace the lightness brought with it.

His boots lost contact with the top of the tower. He rose up, the only thing keeping him from climbing into the sky being the harness that kept him front-to-back against the witch, and the only thing keeping *her* down being the marriage of lodestone and amulet.

The chamberlain moved in and set his hand on the lodestone once more. "Fare well. Death to the enemy of the king." Then he spoke the phrase that stilled the talisman's power.

Immediately Fox and the witch rose. The group on the tower vanished into the dimness, their presence evidenced only as a set of increasingly small circles of lamplight.

The castle and town unfolded below, a tapestry of glowing windows. The surrounding farmlands were sketched in greys and blacks, a glimmer of argent indicating the course of the river.

They reached the point of equilibrium at a level Fox judged to be three times as high as an arrow shot from the mightiest of longbows could reach.

"I could never tire of this," Fox said in awe.

"You could. Trust me," the witch replied. "Now—what was that code phrase?"

"The Snake of the East."

"It would be something like that," she commented. She put her hand on the amulet and repeated the words. The amulet rotated them until they faced east, and began to tug them onward.

Their pace increased until the wind began to whip at their clothing and hair. Gazing straight ahead became unpleasant even through narrowed eyelids. Fox doubted even a falcon could fly so fast, not even when plunging toward its prey.

They travelled in silence for an hour. It would take another hour to reach the eastern boundary of the realm, but even now the terrain was dominated by uncut woods and undrained wetlands.

Her back was no longer chill against him, and he no longer numb. Fox found it impossible not to dwell upon the scent of her hair at the nape of her neck. He couldn't banish the memories of the times when he'd been pressed up against a woman in this way. Nor could he manage to stifle his body's response.

"You compliment me, Sir Foxtread."

"I am glad you take it in that spirit."

"I used to live for the senses. Though sometimes it's hard to recall those times."

"I've heard tales of the old you," he admitted.

"You know so much of me, yet I so little of you," she said. "Have you been in the king's service long?"

"Since I was eleven, Your Highness."

"How did it happen?"

He wondered if he could tell his story were he not pressed so close, his mouth next to her left ear.

"My mother was a whore and then a washerwoman. The only father I knew was the tanner by the river whose bed she warmed. I ran off. I was tired of the beatings."

"And did you kill the tanner later?"

"Perhaps."

"I was seven when my father's wizards began to shape me into what I am. Couldn't have done it if I had been much older. It's tricky enough magic as it is, and rare enough to find a vessel able to receive it at any age. As it was, it took twenty years."

"The first success in two centuries," he said.

"Told you about that, did they?"

"Yes."

"Did they tell you I chose it?"

"I don't see how that could be true. As you say, you were only seven."

"But I was asked, and I willingly swore to do my part. It is quite a thing, for a female to be able to defend the realm."

"And you have defended the realm, Your Highness. Many times."

"True. But it never meant as much as I imagined. Not after the first year."

Fox didn't reply. What could he say?

"How many men have you killed, Sir Foxtread?"

"That's hard to say. Even when I was a boy they had me running through the battlefields hamstringing the horses of the enemy knights and then thrusting my stiletto into the eyeslits of any who fell to the ground. There were many battles. It was just after your brother became king. You remember the wars of expansion."

"But everyone you killed, you killed close up. You could have kept a tally, if it had been your way."

"I suppose I could have."

"I could not possibly say how many have died as a result of my doings," she said in a murmur so soft the wind almost stole the words away. "I have floated over battlefields and returned to tell the commanders which enemy flank was vulnerable. I have dropped naptha inside castles and babies and chambermaids have burned along with the guards."

"Best not to dwell on this, Your Highness."

"How do you bear it? Speaking as one killer to another, how do you do it?"

"There was no purpose to the life I was leading as a tanner's stepson. Now there is."

"Is it as simple as that?"

"I keep it simple, Your Highness. I am the king's poison. I am his garrotte. Any time I am sent out on his business, I may die, so life becomes keen. Right now, when I look down and see how far we are from the treetops, my heart pounds. I feel the flow of blood behind my ears. I know I'm alive."

"And you do not drink."

"No. It would dull the keenness."

"We are made of different stuff, Sir Foxtread."

"I'm afraid so."

They said not one more word more as they crossed into the Lakelands. The homesteads and crossroads communities were invisible to them, the late hour having caused lamps and cookfires to be extinguished, save for a wharf lantern or two left to show the way home to fisherman out in their boats.

Finally they were out over the largest lake of all. Their destination was the keep on the far side. Fox wondered if his intended victim had any inkling of the danger he was in. The rebel had chosen to bide his time in what must have seemed to be an unusually secure stronghold. And so it had been every other time he had taken shelter there. But that was before a spy had succeeded in hiding a lodestone within it.

The silhouette of the keep was looming large when their speed finally eased. They coasted to a halt so gentle the amulet did not even make a noise when it touched the lodestone.

Fox evaluated their position. The spy had done well for them. They were dangling high on the lakeside wall of the fortress, shadowed even from the glow of the newly-risen quarter moon. From this spot the drop was straight down ten stories to the water. The guards had small reason to fear infiltration from this approach. Though Fox and the witch were only a dozen feet below the parapet, they would not be seen.

Fox listened intently, as only someone trained in his art could listen. No one was walking along the battlement. No one was standing in wait, breathing. He uncoiled his rope and soon his noose settled over the nearest merlon. No one shouted an alarm. No one rushed up to cut the rope. He pulled the line taut and wrapped the free end around his hand three times.

Buckle by buckle, slowly so as to make no noise, he released the straps that bound him to the witch. And then he peeled free of her.

As his chest and abdomen lost contact with the skin of her back, the enchantment ceased to have its effect upon him. As she bobbed up a little higher, freed of his weight, he felt the world trying to draw him downward into a plunge, a death he thwarted by his firm grip on the rope, by the support of a tiny ledge beneath one boot, and by the strength of his arm.

He untied her rolled-up cape and let it fall so as to keep the night air off her bare back. The witch had already withdrawn into somber silence, accepting to whatever degree she could that while she was waiting afloat beside the fortress, he would be inside engaging in murder her participation had made possible.

He began to climb.

—o—

He was back only an hour later. He rappelled down until they were level with one another.

"It is done?" she asked.

"The Snake of the East will trouble our land no more."

She nodded in relief.

He did not tell her of the sentry and the unfortunate manservant he had been forced to garrote in order to reach the intended victim's quarters. She did not ask.

"My duty is done, then. Time for our farewell. You have been a true friend, Sir Fortread."

"May it always be so, Your Highness."

"Will you not come with me?"

"No, I will return to the king. He will have need of my skills in the future, and I mean for him to have them at his command."

"You still have to get away from the keep safely, and then find a horse."

"I have endured such challenges before."

"And if my brother suspects you helped me?"

"I have just killed his greatest enemy. I trust he will give me the benefit of any doubts he may harbor."

She put her hand to his cheek. And for the very first time since he had known her, she smiled.

He touched the lodestone and spoke the phrase of release. The talisman let go its grip. She began to rise skyward.

As she cleared the battlement, she put her hand to the amulet. In place of the words that would have taken her back to the king's tower, back to her old life in her aerie of windowless stone walls, she said, "A Haven in the Hills."

The sorcery manifested. She headed off not due west, from whence they had come, but at a northerly angle. Precisely where she was going Fox did not know. He had not been privy to that part of the plan. Wherever it was, a lodestone drew her—a lodestone unknown to the king. Wherever it was, friends waited to receive her like the princess she was.

Fox made his way back up the wall, brimming with a feeling he had never known before. He had taken many lives. How extraordinary to be part of saving one.

A MORSEL FOR THE PLAGUE QUEEN

For a man with a wooden foot, Rayl moved with deceptive grace. Once again Verda failed to anticipate his thrust. The blunt at the end of his rapier struck her practice vest hard, adding to the bruises within her left breast. Too late, she sidestepped, deflecting away his weapon.

"Not good enough," he said.

Verda blew a sweaty strand of hair out of her face, wishing she had tied her braid tighter. She glared at Rayl. It was bad enough that he was so much better than she, but worse when he said it aloud.

He limped back to his spot. She tried to calm her mind, ignore distractions.

She saw he wasn't quite balanced. She charged.

He parried her. As she danced back to avoid his counterthrust, she stepped on the hem of her skirt and went sprawling on her rump.

Laughter came from the trees.

She bared her teeth. The two peasant boys, Gritt and Cauld, hooted at her from their perch on a thick oak bough. Or did until Rayl gagged them with his master-at-arms scrutiny.

At their various positions around the glade, the members of the squad worked hard to suppress their own signs of amusement.

Verda hated having to practice in a skirt. She was better in the boy's hose and tunic Rayl had allowed her to wear during the previous week's drills. But now he expected more. "An assassin will not wait for you to compose yourself," he had lectured. "You must be ready to fight at a moment's notice."

Lately he had taken to sneaking up while she was asleep and emitting a shout, and if she did not vault to her feet in an instant, knife in hand, prepared to meet an attack in nothing but her nightshirt, he would thwack her with his "learning stick" of bundled willow switches.

She stole a few moments of respite by staying on the ground. She didn't understand how Rayl could keep going without showing fatigue. He was ancient. Fifty, he had told her a fortnight after he had been assigned to lead her bodyguards. That was three times as old as she.

"Taking the offensive was the right move," he said. "Try it again."

"Must I?" she puffed.

Rayl sighed. "You are the last line of your own defense, girl. Do you want to be helpless?"

Groaning, she rolled onto her feet. But before straightening, she grabbed a handful of dirt. She flung it at Rayl's face.

He back-pedalled, belly-laughing with approval. She closed in. He cleared his eyes and tried to parry, but her sword blunt reached him, landing with enough force that, in a real engagement, he would have taken a serious wound in the mid-section.

"Better," he said. The other warriors murmured approvingly. In the tree, Gritt and Cauld grunted in astonishment.

Verda didn't let her guard down. That was one lesson she had learned well.

But Rayl did not test her further. When he saw that she was alert, he pulled the blunt off his rapier and sheathed the weapon.

"Catch your breath. Noon is nigh."

He stepped behind her and unlaced her practice vest. As the hardened leather casing fell off her body, and the breeze struck the sweat-drenched cloth of her blouse, the sharp, sudden coolness caused her bruises to throb.

She let herself dwell on the discomfort. Pain was a teacher, Rayl had said. It was also a distraction. She wondered if that might be the real reason Rayl had initiated her into a regimen of self-defense. All she knew was that at that moment, she would rather still be getting thumped with a sword and have boys laugh at her than move on to her next task.

—o—

As the sun filtered down through the leaves from almost directly above, heralding the interval when the magic she must wield was at its greatest potency—Verda strode from the woods onto the tilled part of the farm holding she and her escort of king's men had come to aid.

A small crowd of peasants were waiting expectantly at the edge of a barley field. Verda entered the enclosure of pavilion cloth they had erected for her privacy and removed all her clothes. She donned a knee-length frock of rough burlap and reemerged into the open.

Rayl handed her a spear. He had made it earlier this morning from sapling he had cut down. It was a thoroughly primitive article, its point nothing more than a whittled tip. There was no reason to craft anything better.

She set off into the field.

The squad had taken up sentry positions at regular intervals around the entire parcel. If an attack came, the men would protect her as best they could, but only from threats that came from beyond. The threat within the field was hers alone to deal with.

Her calves brushed against stalks of ripening grain. A good harvest had been shaping up here—enough to cover the king's taxes and still leave the serfs with a bounty for their toil. But up ahead, nearly half the field had been transformed. The crop had sickened and collapsed, leaving a matted terrain of spongy, blackened compost. It stank of sewage. Midges and flies spun in lethargic spirals above the area.

The outline of the sick zone was amorphous. Tendrils threaded outward like mangrove roots. What Verda was confronting was a tumor of the land.

Her prey was the spore from which the ugliness sprouted. The cyst. Strong and well-armed as the twenty warriors surrounding her were, they could not locate it for her, nor survive the encounter.

Her gait faltered as she approached the boundary of the infection. A sulphurous plume wafted over her, making her snort. She forced herself to take a step, then another and another, propelled by the knowledge that her only hope of success was to spend as little time as possible in the blighted zone.

As she crossed the threshold, the air clenched around her, dank in spite of the arid summer day. At noon, the effect was as weak as it got, but it was still enough to force sweat from her pores. Her frock began to cling to her sides below the armpits. Her feet sank in with each step, first only a toe's height, then nearly to the ankles. Only the lightness of her body, the lack of heavy gear or armor, and the interlaced net of fallen grain stalks prevented her from becoming bogged down.

Her throat constricted. Her lungs did not want to fill with the putrid air. She made them do so. The inhalation made her feel as though foulness were taking root inside her chest, but if she didn't breathe, she would pass out, and the blight would claim her.

Now that she was within the boundary, the enchantment that had been placed upon her became active, revealing the proximity and direction of her goal. The cyst lay to her left. It was not in the center of the vileness—that would have been too easy. Too symmetrical. Less evil.

She struggled through the rest of her approach, reaching a place where the earth was slightly mounded, though this was only apparent now that she was close. As she took the last few steps, insects harassed her eyes, tried to crawl into her ears, into her nostrils. The stench increased.

Finally she was close enough. In a swift, sure motion, she thrust into the mound with the spear.

A shriek overwhelmed the buzz of the insects. The spear bucked. She pulled it free before she lost her grip.

A viscous mass, greatly resembling a ball of mucus, emerged from the soil. It oozed a puslike discharge from the wound Verda had made.

She thrust again, this time right at the center.

Another shriek set her eardrums to ringing. Knowing what was coming, Verda threw up her free arm to shield her eyes. The cyst...popped. Sticky, clinging matter exploded in all directions, spattering Verda from head to foot.

Around her on the field, the substance began sizzling, eating into the matted stalks and soil like acid. Both her spear and her frock began to decompose. But the anointment did nothing to her skin and hair save hang there. It revolted her with its texture, its heat, and its odor, but it had no destructive effect.

The shreds of the cyst collapsed. Verda poked the larger flaps of membrane several more times, but did not get a living reaction. She discarded the spear.

Already the flies and midges were drifting away in the wind. The stench was fading. The grain, of course, would continue to rot, but in a natural way, fertilizing the soil. In three or four years, the patch would seem normal to look at, to tread upon, to smell. In a decade, people could safely eat food grown in its soil.

Most important, the area would no longer expand until it consumed the entire holding and those next to it.

Verda wobbled away from the thing she had killed. At first, the droplets that fell from her bubbled and fumed as soon as they hit the ground, then even this lingering element of sorcery ceased. Her frock, which was holding together only because half of it had been shielded from the spray by her body, stopped disintegrating.

Finally she reached the pristine zone. Rayl was waiting there.

"Well done," he said.

Beside him stood the peasants, whose field this was. They included the boys, Gritt and Cauld. The latter did not appear ready to mock her now. Verda almost wished they would, rather than see them cringe in disgust at the spectacle of her.

"Great Lady," said Mott, the landholder, "on behalf of myself, my kin, and all my neighbors, I thank you."

Verda acknowledged him with a nod. It was all she could manage.

"Let's get you cleaned up," said Wreena, Mott's wife.

Verda returned to the enclosure, this time accompanied by Wreena and her teenaged daughter Brigg, a sister of Gritt and Cauld. Verda slipped out of the remnant of the frock. Wreena handed her a block of soap, and then she and Brigg took turns pouring ladlefuls of warm water over Verda. The water came from a cauldron the family had transported to the site on their hay wain.

Viscous strands of ichor and greyish suds flowed off her. She stepped clear of the resultant muck and the procedure was repeated.

Verda appreciated the peasant women's trouble, to heat water for her and bring it out so far from their hearth. The last time she had destroyed a cyst, she had bathed in cold well water. "More," she murmured as soon as the third round of rinsing was done.

Pampering was not something Verda was used to. She would not waste the experience.

—o—

She was still light-headed when the peasants and her bodyguards gathered for supper, but at least she was clean. The aroma of the food even awakened her appetite—just a little.

The meal was served outdoors around a bonfire in the farmyard, for none of the buildings would have accommodated so many visitors. The holding was home to three large families, but their dwellings were hovels clustered against the half-collapsed remains of a watchtower left over from the Forgotten Age. The peasants did not even have a barn, only a pigsty and goat pen. Their grain was stored in root cellars, their hay in stacks in the open fields.

Their hosts proudly served skewers of roast chevon along with brimming bowls of porridge. Verda realized they must have slaughtered a pair of goats for the feast, and wondered how many months it would be until they had meat again, aside from whatever small game might succumb to snares or to the boys' slings.

Many gazes were upon her. She made sure to eat as heartily as she could manage to honor their hospitality—their only material way of showing their gratitude. Much as her bony form needed a little fattening, it was not an easy task. Every time she encountered a cyst, she had to re-learn the desire to thrive.

When everyone had eaten and beer had been served, Mott raised his cup in salute. "To King Takk and his cousin, the noble Verda, a true daughter of Ommero."

A cheer went up.

"Where will you go next, My Lady?" Mott asked. "How long until you return to the palace?"

Verda knew the serf was trying his best to be an amiable host and engage her in as much conversation as someone of his low station could dare, had she been who he thought she was. She could not answer him.

Rayl responded for her, before the pause grew uncomfortably long. "Alas, the Plague Queen is determined to reclaim her realm. She has roamed far and wide, spewing out the sort of abomination you saw destroyed today. Tomorrow we must move on to aid your neighbors at Heather Bluff. From there, we cannot yet know how many more places we must visit."

"May you fare well," Mott said.

"The old tales say Prince Ommero killed the Plague Queen. Is this *another* one?"

The speaker was young Cauld. His mother twisted his ear for his lack of etiquette.

Rayl held up his hand, granting pardon.

"It is a fair question. One that is on the minds of many in the realm, I am sure." Rayl's tone became grim. "What we face is indeed the same being. Evra, the Plague Queen, who ruled these lands until two centuries ago, when nearly all of this great valley was the Fever Swamp, and our people were little more than shepherds and olive growers in the hills. She is one of the bloodwraiths who was unleashed in our world during the Sorcerers' War. It is not possible to truly slay a bloodwraith. Ommero destroyed the suit of flesh she wore. It caused her great agony. It made her unable to wield most of her power, so that when Ommero assumed the kingship and commanded his engineers and laborers to drain the swamp, the effort succeeded, giving us our fine, fertile croplands and noble estates. But it did not kill her. For generations our people described Evra as dead because it was assumed her essence had been sucked back to her dimension, where she could bother us no more. Now we know she hid away somewhere, perhaps in the deepest part of the delta where men never go. She has manifested again. With a corporeal body, her sorcery has its old potency back. So for these past four years, she has laid her hideous spores, trying to turn our realm back into the Fever Swamp."

"Is it true she has killed two of King Takk's sons?"

"It is," Rayl replied.

The peasants murmured apprehensively. A small child hid behind his mother's skirts.

"Evra has a special enmity for the House of Ommero," Rayl continued. "First, to have revenge. Second, because anyone who carries the blood of the man who defeated her is immune to the full effect of her magic, and this enrages her. The princes are only two of the victims. Outside the king's own household, a score of other descendants have fallen. Evra is powerful and she is resourceful."

"But King Takk can kill her, can't he?" asked Gritt. "The way she was killed before?"

It was an even bolder question than his brother's had been. Rayl frowned at Gritt, the way he had frowned at him back in the tree during the sword practice. Gritt cowered.

"The Plague Queen's day of reckoning will come. The king hunts her as we speak. Meanwhile, he has arranged to send his lesser kinsfolk—even fourth cousins, fifth cousins—to such places as this, to destroy the cysts before the land is rendered too sick to be worth saving."

Verda saw the serfs glance at her with new insight, understanding now why they had never heard her name before. They had been too intimidated by the escort of twenty king's guards to confess their ignorance, fearing they would cause insult.

She knew they didn't suspect the rest. Undoubtedly they still assumed she was a figure at court. The truth was, she had never seen the palace, much less been welcomed inside. Long ago, Ommero's youngest daughter had been given in marriage to the first Duke of Riverbend, who gave his own youngest daughter to a favorite vassal, a knight beloved far and wide, but only a marchwarden in terms of rank. Later the warden had needed money, so he made a rich merchant into a son-in-law. The merchant had been a commoner, and so Verda, his granddaughter, was a commoner as well.

Her ancestry had never been significant until those with even a drop of the blood of Ommero in their veins had been conscripted into the war against the Plague Queen.

"Excuse me," she said, standing up. "I am very tired. I would like to sleep now."

Wreena leaped up to show her the way to her accommodations—Wreena and Mott's own straw tick in the loft of their hovel. A cheer followed her away from the bonfire. To Verda, it was an assault on her ears when she only wanted silence and solitude.

Rayl studied her as she passed by him. She avoided his gaze.

—o—

She burst awake to find Rayl with his hands on her shoulders. He was shaking her.

The nightmare—the usual one of drowning in stagnant, scum-coated pool deep in a swamp—lost its grip on her. Her eyes focussed, recognizing the loft. A rooster was crowing, but it was still full dark, the only illumination coming from the lantern Rayl must have re-lit.

Furrows were etched deep in Rayl's forehead. "Breathe deep. Let it pass," he said. He let go of her, letting her sink back onto the mattress.

She tried to let go of the tension. But her heart kept hammering the inside of her ribcage. Muscles ached all over her body. And her left arm itched in a maddening way. It was the worst episode yet.

"I don't know how much longer I can do this," she said.

He raised a finger to his lips. She caught the mouse-stirs from below—cookfires being stoked up, bed pallets being removed from the floor to be stored away for the day. The peasants were awake, and might overhear.

She kept the silence he wanted, but it was harder than it had ever been. She wanted to shout until her outcry echoed from the thatch above her head: *The king cowers in his palace under triple guard. He sends cousins he has never met out to save his lands, to become targets for his nemesis.*

"I'm just a girl," she murmured. "How did it come down to me?"

"If you don't do it, who will?" Rayl whispered.

—o—

It was a mark of her exhaustion that she managed to go back to sleep, if only for one more hour. She awoke to the sound of eggs frying and the aroma of porridge as it bubbled in Wreena's kettle. She stayed still and kept her eyes closed, trying to hoard her strength. She was sure the squad already had their bedrolls packed and would be ready to depart for Heather Bluff as soon as breakfast was over. The prospect of fighting another cyst at noon was unbearable.

Unfortunately the itch on her arm tormented too much to let her linger further. She gave up, threw on her clothes, and climbed down the ladder.

The peasant family curtsied and bowed. "Good morning," she said in as friendly a tone as she could manage given her unsettled mood.

She lifted the door flap and stepped out. The east had buttered, but the sun was not yet peeking above the horizon. The air was refreshingly brisk.

Rayl, as she could have predicted, was the guard stationed closest to the door. "What's wrong with your arm?" he asked in place of a greeting.

Verda realized she had been scratching even while she walked. She turned the arm outward. Now that she was in the light, she saw just how large the irritated area was at the inner elbow, and spotted the pinprick of red.

Rayl's face went pale. "She has found you," he told Verda. He tossed away the mug of tea he had been drinking and shouted to his men: "Battle ready! The Plague Queen comes!"

As always, a third of the squad were stationed at intervals around the holding; they had only to stay as they were in order to do as Rayl commanded. The rest began donning armor, lacing up boots, stringing bows, buckling on scabbards.

Verda vomited the remains of her supper onto the ground in front of her.

All three peasant families burst from their hovels. Rayl held up a hand to quiet their cacophony. "The Plague Queen will be upon us at any moment. Gather everyone inside the watchtower. We will try to fend her off, but you should bring anything that can serve as a weapon. Bring your dogs."

Men and boys rushed to do as he said, while mothers

snatched babies from cribs, and girls rounded up toddlers.

Rayl helped Verda straighten up. He held out her rapier and sword belt. "Remember all we've spoken of. Hope is not gone."

She spat out a final bit of vomit. "Yes it is. You know it is. Hope is for the king in his castle."

"Then be brave." He made her close her hand around the sword grip.

"I'm not ready to die, Rayl. I've barely lived."

"All the more reason to cling to hope," he said. "Now, please, get into the tower."

He assisted her to the place in the ruined wall where the barbican had once been. These days only a gap remained, but most of the rest of the wall was eight or ten or even twelve feet high, a nearly unbroken ring that made it a credible place to attempt a last stand.

Suddenly the northernmost sentry cried out, "Mindless ones!"

Men were shambling out of the woods where Verda and Rayl had sparred with blunted rapiers the previous morning. The newcomers marched straight into the blighted area where she had killed the cyst, the still-repugnant part of the holding that any sane man would avoid.

But these were not sane men. The first rays of day revealed their blank countenances. They were the Plague Queen's slaves—men who had succumbed to her snares, and now had no will of their own.

The sunshine also revealed the swords and axes and pikes in their grips. And one other, far worse thing. The bloodwraith herself hovered in the air, personally directing her army.

Verda screamed.

Rayl covered her eyes and pressed her through the gap, taking her to a spot against the wall opposite the opening, the place that would be farthest from the point of attack.

"No," Verda pleaded.

Rayl stood up to leave. Verda clutched him by the leg.

"I have to command the defense," he said gently. "If I could, I would stay. It has been an honor to know you, Verda of Weaver Crossroads."

"Don't say that. Don't go. Don't die."

Rayl beckoned Mott, who had just appeared with a bundle of long sticks to make into torches. "Keep her close. Protect her as long as you can."

Mott nodded. Rayl hurried away.

"Nooooo..." Verda wept.

The watchtower filled with the rest of the locals. Verda's moans were drowned out by the wails of the children. Rayl ordered archers to the tops of piles of fallen tower stones. It seemed like only a moment had passed before they were nocking and releasing their arrows; the enemy was already that close. It was only a moment more before the first of them fell dead, shot through the eye as he stood above the level of the wall to shoot a second time. Evra's army had its own archers.

The bulk of Rayl's squad gathered just inside the opening, forcing the mindless ones to come at them one at a time. The first attacker flung himself onto the points of the defenders' swords, heedless of his own safety. Before the swords could be pulled from the body, more mindless ones surged forward, and just that quickly, the front two of Rayl's men were speared in their midsections, struck so violently that their chain-link armor gave way.

An insectlike whine rose in pitch and volume. It was maddening in a preternatural way, making the guardsmen stagger and shake their heads, breaking their concentration.

Verda huddled in her spot between two pickle barrels, trembling. Suddenly Mott knelt down beside her. He was holding a lit torch.

"I did not have time to tell the captain..."

"Tell him what?"

Mott handed her the torch and moved the barrel beside her out of the way. Beneath it was a trap door. Mott lifted it, revealing a tunnel.

"The people who built the tower made this. It leads through the hill to a hidden spot in the woods. We will send the children through. But you go first. Your survival matters most."

Verda seized the torch and, rapier clutched in her other hand, plunged into the opening.

The walls hugged close. Diminutive as she was, she had to stoop in order to avoid hitting her head on the roof. The air was stale with the musk of earth and grubs. The torch gave off only enough light to make it seem as though she were vanishing down the gullet of some giant creature.

The screams of men dying faded, replaced by the echoes of her own panting and, somewhere far behind her, the muffled shrieks of small children who did not want to be forced into the passageway.

Only then, in headlong flight, did guilt swell. Rayl and the others were facing death. According to the plan, she was to be with them to the end. But now that she had the unexpected chance, she couldn't stop running.

A gleam of daylight appeared ahead. She threw down the torch, letting it snuff out in the dust. She put on a burst of speed that made her trip and skin her knees, but she was up and going again even before the blood could ooze from the scraped spots.

She burst through the veil of scrub ivy and into the open.

In front of her, a creek babbled. Trees and leaves shaded her. She was so far from the battle she could only hear a faint clang of metal striking metal. She couldn't hear the awful insect whine at all.

She darted across the stream and ran along the far bank. It did not take her perfectly away from the holding, but it kept her under cover of brush and trees. Her other choice was to cut across an open field.

She ran like a hare flushed from its burrow. She might lack girth and strength and training, but speed was one attribute she was blessed with.

She was daring to believe that she might actually be getting away when a sharp blow to her upper back sent her sprawling into a patch of bracken. She landed so hard the wind was knocked from her.

Breathless, she forced herself to spin onto her back. She swung her rapier in a wide arc.

Above her, the Plague Queen flitted back. The sword stroke missed.

Verda would have screamed again if she'd had air in her lungs. Rayl had told her the Plague Queen's current form was nightmarish, but he had spared her the details. The bloodwraith was a monstrous mosquito, its body as long as her own, its wingspan greater than the largest eagle. A swamp mosquito, its abdomen oily and red, the bristles on its legs dripping with greyish scum.

Verda held her sword at the ready. The Plague Queen... laughed. "Spawn of Ommero. You only had the one chance." The mirth and the taunt were decipherable in spite of being rendered in a mosquito-like burr.

All too soon Verda understood what her attacker meant. A numbness claimed her neck, and began spreading down into her body. She reached behind her head and found an oozing place at her nape. Evra had not merely knocked her down; she had stung her.

Verda became so weak the rapier fell from her grip. Soon her arm itself plopped to the crushed bracken. She tried to wriggle away—anything to put more distance between her and the bloodwraith—but her legs were so leaden she could barely divot the loam with her heels.

Evra descended, landing right atop Verda, flicking away the sword with a middle foot.

Verda thrashed as frantically as she could manage, but Evra was barely jostled. At her leisure, she took aim with her proboscis, and thrust it into Verda's neck.

As her blood was siphoned away, Verda grew faint, but not so much that she was graced with unconsciousness. She felt the sharp pinch of the wound, the weight of Evra's body atop her. She could see the giant mosquito abdomen swelling and reddening from the meal.

Evra lifted her head back, pausing at her feast. "Your blood is sweet. I will savor it. I may keep you alive for days, child of

Ommero, and snack upon you when the mood strikes me."

From farther down the creek came high-pitched human cries of terror. The peasant children had emerged from the tunnel. Gritt and Cauld were yelling at their juniors to be quiet and run. Verda moaned, realizing that the youngsters were heading to the spot where she lay, unaware of Evra's presence.

Evra rose into a hover, scanning through the trees. "Oh, good," she said. "My slaves needed some fresh meat for their supper." And she began to laugh again.

The laugh transformed into a screech. Abruptly the bloodwraith began thrashing in midair. She spun in a circle, then crashed to the earth an arms-length from Verda. She writhed there, her movement quickly becoming feeble.

"Your...your blood was *sweet*."

"It had a little something extra in it for you," Verda said. As Rayl had so often told her, she was the last line of her own defense. How she wished he could have been there. She had not played her part quite the way they had pictured, but the goal had been accomplished nonetheless.

Evra crumpled. Her new body, that had taken her two centuries to shape and to inhabit with her essence, twitched a final three or four times, then it moved no more.

—o—

Verda slid into a state of hazy consciousness. She remained aware of pain, of the heaviness of her limbs, of the metallic scent of clotted blood wafting up from her neck. A twig snapped. Gritt and Cauld and a bevy of small children were staring at her and the dead bloodwraith in the crushed bracken. They ran off shrieking.

Eventually—she could not calculate how soon—she heard heavier footsteps. Figures loomed over her. To her astonishment, she recognized Rayl and two other members of the squad. They were bloody and all three moved gingerly, but they did not seem to be mortally injured. At Rayl's command, one of the younger men chopped the giant mosquito body in half with his battle axe.

Rayl knelt down at Verda's side.

"You live. You live," she murmured. Tears welled on her eyelashes and let go, dribbling down her cheeks.

"I do," he said.

"I'm...sorry. I'm sorry I ran."

"Had you not, I would not be here now." His tone held no reproach. Suddenly the pain, the numbness, the certainty of her own death, did not trouble her as they had.

Rayl cradled her head, hissing as his fingers touched the oozing bite at the back of her neck. As he gazed at the other puncture, the crease in his brow grew so deep it stretched from the top of his nose nearly to his hairline.

"It's bad," she said. "I killed her, but she killed me."

"Hope is not lost," he said.

"You always say that, even when you don't believe it."

"I *always* believe it," he replied.

The delirium deepened. Time did not flow; it skipped. At one point, gentle hands were cleaning her wounds with a moist cloth. In the next moment, so it seemed, the surface beneath her was jostling and bumping, and she realized she was being transported on a wagon. Her flesh felt so hot and waxen she felt sure it was melting off her bones.

A blanket was draped over the wagon, screening her from the

sun. The coolness and the dimness appealed to her so much she surrendered to them.

—o—

The next she knew, she was lying in a bed softer than any she had ever before felt.

She opened her eyes. The bed was immense, its posts made of finest rosewood, its canopy draped in fine Southern blue silk. Cut fresh flowers filled Ayr porcelain vases on matching nightstands on either side. The walls were draped in tapestries of superb craftsmanship, depicting key events in the lives of leading members of the House of Ommero.

And in a plush chair, his hair combed, dressed in fine court livery, his face and hands more pristinely clean than she had ever seen, his weapons absent, sat Rayl. His eyes were closed. His head rested on the cushioning. His chest was rising and falling at a steady rate.

She tried to speak. It came out as a cough.

Rayl was instantly and fully awake. He sat up sharply, a warrior ready to deal with whatever he must. As he became oriented, he relaxed and grinned at Verda.

He *grinned*. Verda had never seen him do that before. He picked up a crystal bell from the small table by his chair and rang it. The tone reverberated enchantingly off the ceiling's great wooden beams and panels.

She coughed again. He poured her a cup of water from her nightstand pitcher. She drank without stopping until it was gone.

"There. You look better already," Rayl said.

"I thought I would die."

"It was a near thing. Such a fever you had. It took the skill of the queen's best healers to pull you through."

"What happened back at the holding? How did *you* survive?"

He held up his left arm. Verda saw a partially healed slice that ran halfway from wrist to elbow. It would leave him with another battle scar for his collection. "The attack ceased the moment Evra died. Deprived of her influence, the mindless ones lowered their weapons and simply stood where they were. I am afraid we killed several without need before we realized what had transpired."

"And the peasants?"

"All were saved. We shielded the adults from the horde. The children made it through the tunnel unscathed."

"I saw Gritt and Cauld. I think."

"They found you. You are their heroine, you know. They wanted to run to every holding and shepherd's hut in their whole shire to tell what they had seen. They only gave up the idea when I told them they could help escort your litter to the palace. It's only been three days since they returned to their farm."

"Three...days?"

"You were ill more than a fortnight, and it has been another day since your fever broke."

The wonder of being alive was replaced with something less sweet. "Why did you tell Gritt and Cauld not to tell everyone I what I did?"

"Because they would not have told the right tale."

The speaker was a woman. She had already reached the foot of the bed—Verda had paid only minimal attention to the subtle sounds of a door opening and closing. Her attire, though clearly meant as casual parlor wear, was so resplendent Verda had no doubt of the woman's identity.

Verda deliberately did not make any attempt at an obeisance. "What tale do they tell instead?" she demanded.

"That the king laid a trap for the demon," said the queen, "and when Evra fell into it, Takk was at last able to confront her. He slew her with his own axe, showing himself to be a true heir of Ommero."

"Of course," Verda said bitterly. "And what tale do they tell of me?"

"That you were among the cousins sent into the provinces to kill the cysts. That you did more than that? I suppose there will always be rumors that the king was not present when the Plague Queen perished. There are rumors noted in the old histories that say Prince Ommero was not there when she was killed the first time. But you will tell whoever asks that they should not believe rumors. Nor will you ever speak of Evra dying by means of poison, or of you and the others being sent out as bait, at the risk of your lives, while the king remained hidden in his stronghold."

Verda gritted her teeth so firmly her jaw hurt.

"You want to tell the truth."

"Should I wish to further lies?"

"Lies will be furthered, whether you wish it or no. It is for the best. My husband is like any king; he does not wish to lose face. The people are like any people. They want to believe their leader is mighty. Even as we speak, His Majesty and his retinue are visiting every corner of the kingdom, displaying the body of Evra for all to see. You cannot imagine the rapture and relief his visits bring. You would not wish to see how fearful those same people would be, were they to know the real story, and understand how near the bloodwraith was to success, and how impotent we were against her these four years."

Verda could not understand how the queen could gaze at her so steadily, so unabashed. "Did the king do anything? Was he even the one who came up with the *plan*?"

"No. It was my plan." Yet even that confession did not cause the queen to drop her gaze. "But it was a king's magician who altered your blood. Those were king's men who escorted you, enough of a guard that Evra did not suspect you were bait. Does it matter who takes credit, as long as the realm is saved?"

Verda sighed. "I see. So I am to go back to my fief, and keep my tongue." The last three words burned her throat on the way out.

"Your silence is necessary, but going back to your village? That won't do at all. I need you here."

Verda blinked. "What do you mean?"

"You are a young lady of proven ability and bravery, who wishes to do what is best for her land. You want your contribution to matter. I can give you that chance."

The conversation had taken a direction Verda had not expected. She didn't trust it yet, but Rayl's quiet smile made her willing to hear more. "What is it you're proposing?" she asked the queen.

"As you have seen, there are things the king cannot do, that nevertheless must be done if the realm is to thrive. The real work does not happen in the throne room or out on the parade grounds. It happens quietly, in rooms such as this. Think what you will of Takk, but he understands this. He could have failed to follow my advice of how to lay a trap for Evra, but he heeded what I said. He consulted his magicians. He listened to old comrades such as Rayl. And success was achieved."

The queen took Verda's hand. "The right advice, given discreetly and at the right time, means everything. I want to add another voice to the cause. I am getting on in years. It is time I took on another lady-in-waiting, to learn what must be learned, to ensure when my son comes to the throne, and when *his* son comes to the throne, the administration of the kingdom will go on as it should. Will you accept this honor, Verda of Weaver Crossroads?"

"Me? Live in the palace?"

"Yes."

"What of my family?"

"You may visit them when you like, and they visit you. But I think your mother and father will be well occupied arranging their new estate. And your eldest brother busy with his handsome new merchant vessel. But perhaps your sister will agree to join you here. You will need an aide, if you take on as much responsibility as I hope you will."

Verda looked for hints in the queen's demeanor that would indicate insincerity, but did not see any.

"All I have to do is agree, and this will happen?"

"The estates and the ship will happen regardless, as a reward for what you have done already. And the money, of course."

"The money?"

"We will not mention how much coin you will have to spend as you like. That would be gauche."

Verda felt the urge to cough, and hurriedly sipped more water.

"I wish you to understand. I do not demand that you stay. I offer it. Along with whatever other rewards are within my power to grant. So what do you say? Do you wish to make a difference?"

Verda's glance darted to Rayl, then back to the queen.

Rayl began laughing.

"What's so funny?" the queen asked.

"Hope is stirring. She isn't used to it."

Was that the feeling? All Verda knew was what was awakening inside her was strange and vivid, and she wanted to learn its nature.

"I will answer you in the morning," she told the queen.

THE VAPORS OF CROCODILE FEN

I was raised here in the bog. Not many can say that. Few families have chosen to tie their lives to this peat, to these sulphur mists. Would *you* raise your daughter where crocodiles roam? You have seen for yourself how well the creatures thrive here, where the hotsprings and honeycombed channels cure the river of its snowmelt chill. Their pervasiveness is one of the two things for which this place is famous. The other is the Tale of the Dwarf Rebels.

You have not heard that story? The Duke of the Narrows had defeated all his rivals but one, his younger half-brother, Strawhair. Having barely escaped the battle at Founders Knoll, Strawhair fled to a stilt house deep in the bog. Feverish from wounds, bereft of all but two of his fighting men, Strawhair was undone, but the duke was not satisfied. He tortured Strawhair's vassals, learned of the hiding place, and set out with a contingent of knights to eradicate this last challenger of his claim to the fief.

The duke saw no threat in the marshdwellers. We are not

dwarfs, as the legend would have you believe, but most of my folk are short and slight, the better to propel our rafts over masses of lotus and water hyacinth. The welcoming party cowered before the knights' drawn blades. When the duke ordered a group to ferry him and his contingent to Strawhair's refuge, they complied in all apparent meekness. But once they were deep in the swamp, they leaped into the water and rocked the vessels from below until the duke and every one of his warriors fell overboard. Burdened by their armor, the invaders sank into the muck and drowned. It was a trap of Strawhair's design. His first victory among many. Eventually he reigned over the neighboring duchy as well, whereupon he came to be called Thrame Half-King.

Ah. You have heard that name, I see.

My grandfather told me that his grandfather was one of the men who sent the duke tumbling. But nearly every bogdweller will make a similar claim and swear it is the truth, no matter that the ambushers were rewarded by Strawhair with good farmland and fine houses. Which is another way of saying, they did not linger here among their kin, siring their babies by the glimmer of witchfire upon muskrat dames like my mother. There has only ever been one noble estate here, and it did not originate from Strawhair's grant. It was founded by Lithra, Countess of Orchid Mire.

Lithra had not been born into the nobility, but she was a sorceress of such caliber that many rewards came her way, including this property and its appurtenances. You might say that I was part of the latter. I was ten years old when I was indentured to her as a potion wench.

For eight years I assisted the countess in making her concoctions. She taught me much during that span. Many rich and influential folk craved her services. She needed to accommodate at least some of them lest she give up the trade of wealth and favors she had come to enjoy, but she had wearied of collecting ingredients, extracting their essences, then mixing and measuring everything just so. She would leave the dull parts to me, stepping in when the limits of my skill were reached, or when lesser results might harm her reputation.

Whether her clients wished for a philter of seduction, a salve to cure hairiness, incense to poison a spouse, a tonic to ward off plague, she could usually accommodate them. Yet many left disappointed. They wanted what she had—enduring youth. She had been born when Strawhair still reigned, and yet she appeared no older than twenty.

"That drink requires ingredients that no longer exist," she would tell them. No matter how high the bribe she was offered, her answer was the same.

What she said was the truth, as far as it went. The ingredients did not exist. What she did not say, not even to me until she had to, was that on a given day and in a given place, they *would.*

—o—

My first hint that something was looming occurred as I was reading aloud from Lithra's grimoire deck in her study. The countess was standing by the window. When I reached the bottom of the tablet and looked up, the sunlight caught her face in profile.

Her jowls had slackened. I would not have noticed in dimmer light. The change was slight. As soon as she raised her chin, the looseness vanished. I wondered, had I truly seen it? But then I noticed new moles on her upper shoulder, revealed by the cut of her dress—Lithra loved to display her long, sculpted neck. The moles were small. No more than freckles, really. But they marred what had been, as recently as the previous morning, a swath of unblemished skin.

She turned to me. I quickly restored my gaze to the tablet.

"Why is licorice root included in that potion?" she demanded.

I hesitated. "To mask the taste of the hoar moss?"

She clucked her tongue. "That's not even a good guess. Nothing masks the taste of hoar moss."

I winced.

"There *is* no licorice root in that potion," she scolded. "Not if you want it to work."

I looked again at the line of text. It said licorice root. But I should have known better.

Lithra strode to the sand table and raked it smooth, erasing the previous lesson. "When you know the true ingredient, write it fifty times."

"Yes, m'lady."

She marched out, leaving me to my punishment. I sat at the sand table and began to contemplate what rune I would etch.

It was a familiar place to be. Even after years of study, I made errors. I needed to be able to recognize thousands of ingredients—some of which had several names. I needed to know whether to apply them as powders or shavings, hot or cold, for inhaling or for swallowing. Hardest of all, I had to recognize which parts of the instructions in her grimoire were rendered in code. No elixirist writes down his or her lore in such a way that parties uninvited may make free use of it. Fail to recognize the cipher, and a remedy becomes a poison.

I wrote nothing in the sand. I could not concentrate. *Lithra was aging.*

—o—

Over the following week, Lithra grew agitated to a degree I had never before seen. She had always been quick-tempered, but she had the cook whipped for over-salting the soup. When a footman stepped on her hem as she dismounted from a carriage, she threatened to have him castrated. Knowing how his predecessor had ended up, he pissed himself on the spot.

She was quick to snap at me when I arrived in the courtyard the next morning for our daily stroll.

"About time you arrived."

I was startled to see her there. I was in fact early. The countess usually lingered at breakfast—a meal sometimes not taken until noon.

I curtsied. "Your pardon, m'lady."

She held her body stiffly. Her eyes were bloodshot. Had she not slept? Nor eaten?

She launched herself down the main garden path. With my shorter legs, I had to scurry to keep up. I found myself staring at the nape of her neck. The hair was grey at the roots, and the skin cobwebbed by fine wrinkles. By now, she looked to be at least sixty.

Or perhaps only fifty. She seemed older because she had grown plain. I had not realized before that the magic that maintained her youth was also responsible for her beauty.

I glanced back, anticipating the company of servants or one of the guests the countess sometimes invited to keep her amused, but no one emerged from the manor. Soon we could not even see the building through the foliage.

"You have seen the changes in my appearance," she said.

The statement came without warning. I trembled as I answered. "Yes, m'lady. I have."

"All will be well. I need another dose of the Wine of Consorts."

"The —" I tripped on the raised edge of a flagstone, and nearly fell. "Did I hear you say —?"

"The Wine of Consorts. One of the Elixirs of the Numinous Mages."

"Everyone says the art of making those was lost."

"That is what they say."

Yet Lithra had mastered at least one of them. She was telling me she was at the level of the sorcerers of legend.

"I can hear your mind working," Lithra said. "You are remembering the nature of the great potions."

She had read me. Just as existence is expressed in solid, liquid, and gas, the highest magic bestows its abundance in three aspects—the internal, the external, and the threshold between. Plainly, in Lithra's case, the bounty of the internal aspect was her enduring youth. Her body had been altered so that it no longer suffered the effects of passing time. Her beauty was surely the bounty of the threshold. It wasn't that her form itself had grown lovely, but a glamour affected the way observers perceived it.

That left the bounty of the external. "You have some kind of power over the world around you, or over the people around you," I said.

"Yes. But if you haven't guessed what it is, I shan't tell you. I am already sharing more than I care to." She extended her hands.

"Do you see how they shake?"

"Yes." I had already noticed the tremors.

"I need you to be my hands. I can't trust my grip. Were it not for that, I would not have brought you along. Be thankful you learn anything at all today."

"Yes, m'lady."

It was an odd place to be in. My fingers were short, like the rest of me, and the countess had on occasion been displeased with my dexterity.

"Is it always like this?" I asked. "Do you have to endure this decline?"

"It was safe to take a new dose weeks ago. It is because of my partner that the timing is so inconvenient." She spat into the hedge. "May he dine on goose dung at every meal."

"Your partner?"

We stopped. Lithra fixed her stare upon me. "You will repeat none of what I am about to tell you, do you understand?"

"As you command, m'lady."

At the quickness of my answer, she grew more calm.

"The Wine of Consorts is called that because it must be made from a pair of catalysts—one supplied by a female, the other by a male. In a few minutes we will rendezvous with my ally. I would be happy never to have to look at him again, but I do not have that option."

We continued on in silence. I was too stunned to dare more questions. Lithra was the last person I would have expected to have a partner of any sort, let alone one whose contribution was so key to her success and station in life.

She ignored the usual meandering garden paths and mazes

and led us onward in as straight a route as we could take toward the edge of the estate, where it melted into the bog. The groomed landscape fell away. We shifted to a gamekeeper's track, a narrow thread of native clay that forced us to lift our skirts to make it through the nettles and berry brambles. The stench of simmering peat grew stronger.

"Do you smell the frogs?" my pa used to say as we returned from our regular treks to the market henge. Lithra's manor house was surrounded by garden flowers and every room scented with bouquets or spiced candles. It was only when I ventured out into this amphibian miasma that I felt at home.

The morning sun was banishing the mists as we reached the end of the path. Ahead lay an expanse of lagoons, shallows, drowned trees, islets, and brush. Slightly to our left a short pier thrust into the deeper channel that bounded this fringe of the marsh. A dinghy was tied to it. Standing on the dock, arms folded and head high, as if he were commanding the gloom to lift, was a large man.

Our movement made no real sound that I heard, but he turned toward us immediately, his right hand darting to the hilt of his sheathed sword. He moved like a fighting man.

He relaxed as he saw who had come. He removed his nondescript travelling cloak and tossed it, along with a campaign duffel, into the boat.

The attire he had revealed was far from nondescript. His shirt was finest silk. His tunic was linen, embroidered with such intricate detail it must have taken a seamstress months to complete the needlework. Many of the colors were more vivid than can be teased from plant dyes, requiring sorcery to achieve.

A warrior he might be, but he was no common soldier. Even at this distance, I recognized his likeness from the proclamations his scribes and messengers had distributed through the land. He was Obur. The King.

"*He* is your partner?" I gasped.

"Yes," the countess replied.

I suppose I might have guessed, if I'd had more than a few minutes to speculate. There were only a few dozen known immortals in the land, and surely her partner had to be one of them. But the *king*?

His gaze settled upon me as we approached. I was unaccustomed to such scrutiny from a male. I felt as though my gown and shift had evaporated, leaving me naked in front of him. The feeling was not unpleasant.

"Who is this young fawn?" he asked.

"My potion wench."

I curtsied. He smiled. I blushed.

"Let's be done with this," the countess declared, clambering down the ladder and into the dinghy.

"After you," the king said.

My hand trembled as I took his. He held me securely as I lowered myself down. I felt...royal.

"Control yourself," the countess snapped. "He's just a man."

Obur began untying the knots that secured the vessel to the dock. "She knows that's not true." He winked at me. Despite what my mistress had demanded, I blushed again.

"Stop smiling," Lithra told me.

And instantly, my lips flattened. Suddenly. As if of their own accord.

All at once, I understood why.

"That was foolish of you," the king told Lithra as he stepped into the dinghy and gave us a push away from shore. "Now she knows."

For eight years, I had obeyed Lithra unfailingly. When she was harsh—which was nearly all the time—I saw her venom as justified. When she treated servants and visitors poorly, I saw it as their fault, and—though my opinion was of course never solicited—I took her side.

Loyalty. That was the final gift the Wine of Consorts had given her. She commanded the loyalty of those around her. Only now, with the magic growing weak, could I even summon the perspective needed to be aware of the compulsion I had been under.

"You be silent," the countess told the king. But he just laughed. That was when I understood the rest—he was immune. He was the one person who could freely choose to be disloyal to her.

Obur took the center bench and picked up the oars. My mistress and I faced him, side by side on the aft bench.

"Well?" he asked.

Lithra pointed. "That channel. Keep to the north as we skirt the mangroves."

So even Obur did not know where we were going. This did not surprise me. It would not have been like Lithra to keep her catalyst within her own manor, where a thief—or an untrustworthy partner—might succeed in locating it. It was hidden more elaborately than that.

The king propelled us on with steady, powerful strokes. We rounded the first bend and the dock vanished behind the mangrove tangle. Ravens called out to warn of humans penetrating the marsh. Turtles abandoned their logs as we approached, to hide in the clouds of algae.

"You've looked better," Obur commented.

Lithra bristled. "I have you to thank."

He chuckled. He stroked his close-cropped beard. It was shot with grey, but only a little. The elixir's grace had not yet abandoned him as much as it had Lithra.

"Perhaps you should have inhaled more deeply last time we were together," he said.

"If I failed to do so, it was because I was holding my nose at the need to be next to you."

"Have care, my orchid in the mire. Or I will think you do not love your king."

"Spare me your blathering," she replied.

A muscle in his jaw twitched, and for an instant, I thought he would pick up an oar and pound her across the skull. Nevertheless his voice was mild as he said, "Your wench wonders how you keep me coming back each time, when you nurse me on such sour milk."

Hair rose on the nape of my neck. He had precisely described how I viewed their bickering. Could he see within me?

Yes. That must be it. People said the king could sense what vassals and courtiers were sincere in their support of him, and that he had an uncanny ability to ferret out traitors. Some believed this insight sprang from a magical source, like his youthfulness. It appeared they were right. It seems the Wine of Consorts had given him the ability to see the true desires and opinions of those around him—his bounty of the external.

Lithra, though, was opaque to him. That irked him.

Surely at one time they had been on good terms. Had time

alone changed their attitudes? Or was it that Lithra couldn't bear the thought of someone she couldn't sway, and he couldn't bear the uncertainty of not knowing if a person near him was arranging to betray him?

All I could do was stare at the power of the king's hands as he gripped and pulled on the oars, and know I would be afraid of attempting to betray such a man. If I ever did and the plan went awry, he would be the most dangerous of enemies.

He studied me. I saw him ferret out my mood, sense my conclusion. He smiled again.

And then he frowned at Lithra. Did she have some trap in mind for him? If so, I didn't know. And therefore, Obur couldn't know, either. It was her secret to have.

"We are going very far in this time," Obur observed after an hour of threading through the lacework of navigable channels. I heard suspicion in his tone.

"I am just following the scent," she replied, "and it has led us this way. It's not much farther. I can tell we're close."

In fact, another quarter hour dragged by. But then, as we rounded a cluster of cattail reeds, Lithra let out a pent-up breath.

"There."

Ahead lay a fallen cypress, one broken, half-rotted limb jutting well above the waterline. From a beetle niche grew a large, strikingly handsome bog lily, its stalk strung like foxglove with blooms, their hue saffron near the crest, deepening to copper at the base. The flowers were like cups, and each hung low, bowed down by unnaturally heavy loads of nectar.

As well as I knew the swamp, I had never seen such a flower.

"It blooms only when I need it to," Lithra explained to me,

with not a little pride in her tone. "And never in the same part of the bog."

It was ingenious. Most of the time, she had no need to hide or to guard the catalyst, because it simply didn't exist.

Obur ceased paddling, letting the boat ease to a gentle drift. This was enough to bring us right under the jutting branch. The king took hold of a knobby projection of the tree trunk and held us in place.

Lithra reached into the campaign duffel Obur had brought and withdrew three items—a flask, a funnel, and a chalice. She put the funnel into the mouth of the flask.

"Tip out the contents of the blooms," she said, handing me the items. They fit together so snugly that it was as if they were one piece. "And need I say? *Be very careful.*"

I made my way to the prow. I had grown up riding in boats such as these and my balance was good, but nonetheless I concentrated on my steadiness. The lower blooms of the stalk were right at the height of my bosom. I decided to begin with those.

A butterfly sailed in. It hovered as if to sample the lily's provender, but it had no sooner come close enough to smell the full aroma than it shot away as if bitten.

I realized gnats and midges were no longer dancing around my face as they had throughout the journey. They were keeping at least four or five feet away from the flower. I saw none of their drowned carcasses in the pools of nectar. Nor any pollen or other impurities.

I tipped a bloom. Four or five drops of syrupy amber liquid fell into the funnel. I realized it would be a lengthy process. The bloom, the largest, was no larger than a pinkie thimble.

A searing pain, like pepper juice in a knife cut, soaked into my index finger and thumb, where the stickiness of the nectar clung. I blew air, but it only served to spread the stickiness a bit further, and added to the agony.

"Yes," Lithra said coolly. "I always hated that part. It's difficult not to get a little on one's skin. Don't be a baby. It will cause no permanent damage."

"You might have warned her," Obur remarked.

"Nothing teaches like experience," the countess replied.

I tried to be even more careful as I harvested the second and third blooms, but a trace more liquid touched my skin. I stifled a whimper. I was sure blisters were rising.

I wondered how something so caustic could be swallowed. Did it become palatable upon being combined with Obur's catalyst?

Abruptly, the answer came to me. One did not drink it. One breathed the fumes.

I said nothing. I was certain I did not want Lithra to know I'd guessed this aspect of the process.

"Well, child," she said. "Do not sit there chewing your curls."

I went back to work, trying to lose myself in the task so as not to notice the discomfort as much. Finally, when more than half the flower's yield had been depleted, Lithra said I had gathered enough.

She accepted the flask from me with care, conscious of her unsteady grip. There wasn't much opportunity to spill any, however. She immediately raised the flask to her mouth, exhaled into it, and tightened the cap.

The flask began to glow—not to the eye, not so that any non-mage would notice a difference, but I had no trouble sensing the aura. From the nods of satisfaction from Lithra and Obur, they perceived it even better than I. Within a few more minutes, Lithra's catalyst would be ready to be combined with Obur's.

How like her, to hide her treasure not only in place and time, but to require one last manipulation on her part to bring it to full strength.

"Your turn," the countess told the king.

He chuckled. "We will see. You might have to be patient."

"Perhaps this time you will choose a different benefit," Lithra grumbled. "One that will make this process easier."

"You would love to see me weakened. No. I will keep the same set of gifts. They have served me well. And being patient will do you good. Spirits know you don't get much practice."

Lithra shot him one of the glares I had borne the brunt of over the years, though the puffiness of the bags beneath her eyes reduced the intensity of it. She tapped her finger against the flask. "Get on with it."

Obur drew his dagger. I hiccupped at the sight, but he did not point it at either of us. He splayed his thumb on the bench, nail side down, and placed the tip of the weapon in the center of the fleshiest part.

He pressed down hard.

His skin held. The knife did not penetrate.

"Hair in my soup would be more use than you," Lithra complained.

Obur shrugged. To me, he explained, "When the magic fades, it goes quickly. But until then, it is as strong as if I had just taken a dose."

"What were you trying to do?"

"His blood is the catalyst," Lithra said.

Obur grinned. "Can you think of a better way to keep it safe?" He jabbed his palm with the dagger. Again, the tip would not penetrate. The bounty of the threshold protected him. The tales of his invulnerability in battle were well-known.

"The sea folk raiders once coated their swords with oils their shamans swore would let them cut me. They tried and they tried. I killed two-thirds of them, and told the others to go back and kill their shamans. I'm told they took my advice."

To pass the time, he told other tales. Lithra sighed and rolled her eyes. After he had described his plans to seize the mines of the southerners on his next campaign, he handed me the dagger and laid his thumb down again.

"Put all your weight into it," he told me.

I was not sure I, small as I was, could press any harder with all my weight than he could with his one arm, but I took the knife, set it on his thumb, and bore down.

At first, the skin held. Then the very sharpest part of the tip sank down a fraction more. A bead of blood formed.

"That will do," he said. He took back his knife. "Hold out the chalice."

I did so. He held his thumb out and squeezed three drops into its gleaming gold receptacle.

The power in the drops radiated over me. It made me sway. Obur liked that.

But I kept the chalice extended.

"No more is needed." Obur said. "Unlike some, my potions are *concentrated*."

Lithra sniffed. "You just don't like to bleed."

They would have kept sniping at each other, but I interrupted them. "That was not enough," I told the king.

"Eh?" he asked.

"You will need more," I repeated, my voice failing as I reached the last word and realized to whom I was speaking.

"How could *you* possibly know that?" Lithra asked. "Let me see, child. Be prepared for a strapping when we return to the manor." But as I held the chalice to her nose and she inhaled, her brows rose.

She scowled at Obur. "More, fool. Unless it's your intent to ruin the spell."

Brows furrowed, Obur checked for himself. He grunted. "So it seems."

He squeezed out one more large drop. "There. That will do." He pressed the chalice closer to me. "Do you agree?"

"Yes. This is enough," I said.

Obur chuckled. "It's not like you to have such a talented assistant, Lithra my sweet."

"She is more gifted than I guessed," the countess admitted. I knew that sour tone. I had not won a reprieve from the strapping.

"There is more, though," Obur said. He was radiant with cheer as he spoke. "Did you know she craves to take your place?"

My heart began to pound. I turned to Lithra, and saw her eyes widen. It was the last expression she would ever wear. In a single efficient move, Obur stood, drawing his sword as he came up. He whipped the blade sideways. Lithra's head tumbled off her neck into the water. It disappeared into the duckweed and flotsam.

I screamed while Lithra's body teetered and spasmed, blood spurting from the severed neck. As calm as a cat on a pillow, Obur snatched the flask of nectar from her fingers before her thrashing could send it flying.

My screaming lasted until after the body had gone limp and flopped to the bottom of the dinghy. Then I began to sob.

"I didn't mean...I didn't want...what have I done?" The words burned as they came out.

I was a murderess. Obur had seen within my heart. It was true, I had longed to be in Lithra's place. To be mistress of a fine house, my life fixed with riches, beauty, admirers? I had always wanted it.

"You will get over it," Obur assured me. "You will thank me, soon enough. Here. Hold this while I deal with the dregs."

He handed me the flask. Somehow I summoned enough composure to grip it securely.

Obur hefted the body onto the gunwale. Another shove, and it would fall overboard. But in that moment, all the weight of it was at one end of the boat, along with the weight of Obur and his accouterments. Before I gave it thought—before Obur could sense my intent and move to thwart me—I flipped backward into the water.

When I surfaced, I saw an upside-down dinghy. The water beyond it was churning. Obur's head and arms shot into view. He thrashed about, eyes wild.

"I will feed you your own toes!" he roared. I remembered the stories of how he dealt with captured enemies, and I nearly vomited. He had not been pulled to the bottom by heavy armor like the Duke of the Narrows and his men. Of course not. Obur did not wear armor. His skin was all the protection he needed from blade or arrow.

Somehow, terror did not paralyze me. While he tried to work his way around the dinghy to get at me, I let go of the chalice, ripped open my bodice and wriggled out of my servant's gown. Buttoning the flask into the lady's friend pocket of my shift, I launched into the fastest swimming stroke I knew.

When I had fled a full skipped-stone length of distance, I dared to glance back. Obur was still next to the boat. He had dispensed with his cloak and was trying to remove his boots, but the weight of his remaining garments sent him under whenever he turned his attention away from treading water.

Any swamp girl learns to swim well. The king, like most folk of our realm, where local waters usually run cold, had obviously never learned to swim at all.

I aimed for the one speck of dry land I had spotted while we were approaching the magical flower. I knew I had to reach it without delay. Dark reptilian forms were converging from the right and the left. I hoped they would ignore me, tasty morsel though I was, and head for Obur, who was still in water crimsoned by Lithra's blood.

A tangle of lotus vines suddenly blocked my way. I knew them as a type that grows only along banks, not in open water, so I thrust my feet down. Finding I could wade, I fought my way through the tangle onto land.

A stirring in the vines in my wake alerted me. I sprang high. Jaws snapped right behind my heels. I sprinted forward and began clambering up the twisted ropes of a strangler fig tree. The tree shook with the impact of a large body. Only when I had reached a branch in its heights did I look down.

A crocodile was leaning on the tree at its base, gazing up at me with what I felt sure must be hope that I might tumble from my perch. Splatters of mud, flung by my scampering feet, dotted its snout. It opened its mouth, and I saw a piece of torn cloth in its teeth. At just that moment, I became aware that the breeze was wafting freely over my bottom. I reached back. My hand came away covered only by mud and swamp scum—and maybe a bit of crocodile saliva—but no blood.

Gradually, my heart ceased pounding, and my breathing steadied. The whole time, the crocodile regarded me. Only when it determined I was not going to plummet into its maw did it stalk back to the water, emitting an almost doglike snort.

Once through the lotus vines it swam with lethal purpose to join its companions near the overturned dinghy.

The spot was a chaos of churning water, thrashing crocodile tails, and bloody foam.

"When the magic fades, it goes quickly," he had said. With luck, he was already dead. If not, at least he was too preoccupied to deal with me. I was determined to make good on my reprieve, and find places to hide where even a man with a king's resources would not find me.

—o—

It took me a quarter of an hour of sloshing across brackish channels and crossing isthmuses of matted vegetation to reach one of the larger islets I knew I would find in the interior of the bog. The whole way I kept alert for crocodiles. Now, finally, that danger was receding. Reaching a spot well clear of the bank, where there was no brush to hide a large predator, I exhaled the terror I'd been hoarding.

Behind me, water sloshed. Something parted the reeds.

I spun around. The fear plunged right back into me.

Obur stood at the edge of the islet. His grin was all teeth.

His clothing was in rags, and what still held together was red and sticky. His skin was no better. He was oozing blood from dozens of punctures and bleeding freely from several gashes. But clearly, his magical invulnerability had not entirely forsaken him. His attackers had not been able to tear him to pieces, nor had they been able to hold him under and drown him.

"Do you know what it takes to fight off crocodiles?" he growled. "You simply kill enough of them that the living decide they would rather feed on their dead brethren than bother with you anymore."

He had lost his sword and his dagger in the struggle, and his right hand was one of the many parts of him that had been badly gnawed. He reached out with the left—an appendage easily capable of throttling the life from me if I let him get within range.

"Now," he said, pointing to the place where my shift bulged from the presence of the flask, "we will finish our business. Don't worry. I'll let you live. One good whiff of the elixir and I will heal completely. How could I stay angry with you after that?"

I turned and raced away.

He snarled. I heard his heavy footfalls as he pursued me. He was gaining. His long legs gave him the advantage in a footrace.

But ahead was the reason I had come here. A large cypress tree rose at the far edge of the islet. A circular platform awaited thirty feet up its trunk. At the same level, a stout rope was anchored, with a pair of thinner, parallel ropes attached higher up. The lines crossed over to a tree rising from the shallows to the west.

I would like to think a squirrel could not have scaled that cypress as quickly as I did. There were no branches down low. I had to shimmy up. But my brothers had taught me well. I was too high for Obur to grab by the time he reached the spot.

Now I had the advantage. I was far lighter than he, and I was not wounded. Reaching the platform, I began scurrying across the main rope, lightly grasping the thinner lines for balance. I was nearly halfway across the gap by the time Obur finished climbing.

He tried shaking the ropes, but the main one was too thick, and the others too taut to let him succeed. Livelihoods depended on maintaining this arboreal highway, for many valuable parts of the bog are inaccessible even by rafts and canoes. If he had been able to use his sword, he might have been able to sever the lines. As it was, he was forced to continue the chase.

Below us, a pair of crocodiles raised their heads off their sandbar and regarded us with interest. One of them opened its jaws. At the sight of the teeth, sweat burst from my palms, but soon I was past them and, breathless and trembling, reached the next platform.

Obur was leaving a bloody handprint behind each time his right hand gripped the guide rope. He was making better progress than I had hoped, his natural agility compensating for his inexperience.

I hurried on. From tree to tree we went—platform to platform through the mid-canopy. I was faster. Bit by bit my lead increased. The great danger was that I get careless and slip. I made sure not to go so fast I let that happen.

Obur, on the other hand, threw caution to the wind and pushed harder. Gradually I understood. At least one of his wounds was deep. He was bleeding to death. If he did not catch me soon, he never would.

Finally I was an entire rope-length ahead. I paused at a platform, ready to launch myself onward, but I saw that Obur had stopped at the preceding one.

His breath was coming hard and ragged. He held the tree's bole for support.

"Wench!" he cried. "You don't want to flee. Stop and think.

What's done is done. You can't bring Lithra back to life. You must think of yourself now. Don't you want to live forever? I know you want it. Cooperate with me, and you will have it."

He had realized the only way left to catch me was with persuasion. It wasn't a bad strategy. He was right in believing that I wanted the bounties of the Wine of Consorts.

But I could not get the image from my mind of Lithra's head sailing off her shoulders into the mire. And I had heard the stories of Obur. They called him the Bloody.

"What will you do, if I save you?" I asked.

"I will give you what you desire. What more do you need to know?"

"No. What will you *do*? For yourself? What will you fill the years with? What will you accomplish?"

He brushed away flies from his face. Drawn by the blood, they were nagging him incessantly. By his delay, I knew just how much his power had faded. He was trying to look within me, to see what answer I wanted to hear, and then he would say it aloud. He could no longer do so. Instead, he had to guess.

"I will do what I have done all along. I will make my realm greater. It is my destiny. Share it with me. I would like that."

He had such a seductive tone. It was said that for all his love of battle and conquest, he had never forced himself on a woman. I saw how that could be true.

But he had given me the wrong answer.

"It is often said, the people of this land were happier before you came to rule," I said.

He tried to rise, to come after me again. He did not have the strength.

"You doom yourself," he snarled. "Can you not see that?"

"I will have as much as I had before," I said. And more, because it would be a better world, with him gone from it.

He pleaded for another hour, whenever he rallied enough to regain consciousness. I cannot say it was easy to keep to my choice. I cannot say I did not continue to be tempted. But my resolve remained intact long enough. I was, after all, of Dwarf Rebel ilk. We choose our dukes and kings with care.

Finally the blood loss had its effect. Obur died there on the platform, hugging the tree.

—o—

Only when the flies were crawling over his distended tongue and moving in and out of his open mouth without any reaction from him, did I realize I might not have to forego the riches he had dangled in front of me. After all, blood was still oozing from him—blood that might yet be able to be a catalyst for the Wine of Consorts.

I retrieved the flask from the pocket of my shift. It still glowed with its eldritch energy.

Tentatively, fearing that Obur might jump up after all and seize me, I crossed the rope bridge to his platform.

Up close, I was able to perceive that his blood had not yet lost its magical potency. True, the power was fading, but only as fast as his body was cooling. I looked about, and as expected, found that the platform was equipped with a cooking pot, a brazier, and charcoal—swamp folk often spend days at a time on their foraging expeditions. I squeezed blood from his wounds into the pot until I was sure I had enough. It took far more than four drops, but that was no problem. I added the contents of the flask.

The elixir quickened.

In the end, I had to heat the mixture like tea in order to inhale enough of the fumes. I suspect Lithra and Obur would have found that step unnecessary. But it worked. I felt the energy radiating from my lungs into the rest of me.

I shoved Obur's corpse from the platform. Descending, I dragged it to the edge of an embankment and let it tumble into the water. It was only right that Obur and Lithra end up together, even if it had to be in the bellies of crocodiles.

Back on the platform, I studied the dregs of the elixir, learning what I could of its nature. I saved what did not steam away, but the dregs, once cool, became inert. I understood the one dose might be all I would ever enjoy. The effects would eventually fade. In ten years? Twenty? I did not know.

In the meantime, the enchantment manifested. By the time I made it out of the marsh and back to the manor house, I was transformed.

I was eighteen. I have not grown older. I doubt you are surprised that I chose endless youth as my bounty of the internal. Who would not want that? And in truth, I am not sure I could have influenced the magic to produce a different result, because the internal aspect is not entirely determined by reason and calculation. My body chose for me, seeking survival above all else.

Second, I chose beauty. I could not help it. I was like Lithra in that regard. I had no love of being plain.

The third bounty, regarding the aspect of the external, now there was where I applied what wisdom I could muster. I had carefully contemplated my options while harvesting Obur's blood.

I did not need to have influence over people. I make friends easily. I had no desire to see their secret desires or to coerce them to loyalty. Instead, I gave myself power over magical lore. As I pored over Lithra's grimoire deck of tablets and unfurled her collection of arcane scrolls, passages that I needed would catch my eye, and I would study them until I grasped the implications hidden between the words. I was drawn to particular shelves in the libraries in particular cities where I would find the right page of the right volume to bring forth critical information I otherwise lacked. I would succeed in locating the right mages with whom I could bargain for advice or written materials that had other elements of what I needed.

It took me less than three years to achieve the first of my two great goals. By then I had the knowledge necessary to create a viable catalyst for the Wine of Consorts. That is, I could make the female half. With a little practice, I found I could do it as well as Lithra, if not better.

The rest was far harder. If it had been easy, others would have done it earlier in history. But after many years, I have achieved the second goal. I know I can teach a male adept of even moderate magical talent to craft the other catalyst.

And so now we are here, my sweet man. Now you understand what it is I have to offer you. Tell me, what gifts would you have? What suite of three powers? Think carefully, for much depends upon your answer.

BEARING SHADOWS

When the child quickened inside her, Aerise made a pilgrimage all the way to the cairn of the First Woman, high on the bluff west of the village, and left a serving of wine from the sacred cask as a token of esteem.

The pregnancy advanced smoothly. No swollen feet. Only a little clenching in her lower back. Aerise took it as an omen. Unlike her first two offspring, this child would enjoy a full life. Week by week, the ripening grasses obscured the small graves Aerise's husband had dug on the far side of their garden. The dark sense of loss grew fainter in her memory.

Her mother was constantly at her side, patting her near-to-bursting belly, helping to chew deerhide to soften the new carrying sling Aerise had fashioned, and offering suggestions on the decoration of the child-braid Aerise would soon have the right to wear. Something with wild boar tooth, perhaps, to fend off the god of Death.

"Perhaps," Aerise replied, knowing she would in fact use

mussel shell, because she loved the river.

On the day things changed, the two of them were on the verge of that river, sitting on a log. Out in the fields, a bored mule pulled a cart down a row. Villagers' harvest knives flashed, cutting stems. Bunches of grapes vaulted through the air, to land on the ever-mounting load. Aerise's husband Duran toiled in one of the crews, adding his clear voice the vintners' chant. Aerise and her dam, shaded by a huge old oak, fulfilled their part of the great communal enterprise by honing the edges of blades the pickers had dulled over the course of the morning.

All was in its place. Soon it would be her child's place. Nine Vineyards had endured in its little valley for three centuries. The plague years had not emptied its fields. The invasion of the Horsemen had not swept it away. Aerise pictured a time three hundred years hence when her descendants would lovingly regard full vats of grapes ready for the crush, and would take their offerings to the shrines on the bluff to commemorate the lives of all the forebears who had cared for this land.

"You are not too hot?" her mother asked, startling her from her reverie.

Such a question. This deep into pregnancy, Aerise's flesh all but simmered. But the oak's leaves hung thickly overhead and a breeze was ruffling her hair, its cool breath promising fog in the night.

"I am fine."

But her mother's brow remained furrowed. "I will soak a cloth for your head," she persisted.

"There is no need," Aerise told her, but her mother was already up, unwinding her sash. The older woman slipped between the curtain of acacia fronds and disappeared over the lip of the riverbank. A few moments later Aerise heard water sloshing, followed by the splatter of drops on cobblestones as her mother wrung out the excess. Despite her protest, Aerise found herself anticipating the cool kiss of the cloth. She set aside the harvesting knife and whetstone, relaxed, and shut her eyes.

"Ahhh-oh!"

Aerise flinched. Her mother stood rigid a few steps away, the wet sash fallen onto the litter of acorns and oak twigs. She looked as aghast as if she had returned to find Aerise strung up and gutted.

"What is it?" Aerise tried to rise, but her balance eluded her. She reached out for assistance, but her mother whirled about and sped toward the workers in the field.

Plopping back down on the log, Aerise finally looked down. And discovered for herself that when the First Woman had granted her wish that her womb be filled, the great ancestress had not been showing favor.

—o—

That night, the great lodge of the village was so full the odor of humanity nearly overrode the reek of fermented grapes emanating from the vats along the walls. Everyone had crowded in: The wisemen and the women's council. Laborers from Creekside and Twin Rock, newly come for the harvest. Her siblings. Her mother. Her husband.

She studied the onlookers. There was her friend Dala, who had come of age with her, been married the same month, both to younger sons of the former headman. Dala averted her gaze.

Others glared at her. She saw disbelief. She saw shock. In the dimness, what had been so difficult to accept was now impossible to ignore. Radiance poured from her abdomen, barely diminished by the presence of her maternity cloak, a brightness to rival the glow of the oil lamps on the walls. The light of her child, showing itself to be the get of a shadow man.

Irony, that the adults of the Cursed Folk could walk the land so invisibly, and yet their unborn announced themselves so plainly. It was the sorcery coming into their bodies that did it, so the bards maintained. When it manifested, the babes-in-womb were unable to contain the gleam of their own power.

The headman took his place in front of the sacred cask, and raised his hands to silence the murmuring. "Aerise, Daughter of Makk," the elder rumbled, any pity he may have had erased by his need to be a leader, to declare what must be declared. "Your crime is apparent to all with eyes to see. You will bear the penalty. You will leave us forever. Your name will not be uttered again within this valley."

The headman turned and showed his back to her. The other wise men, and then the council of women—ultimately, anyone of status within the community—did the same.

Aerise's mother and sisters huddled toward the rear. Her mother sobbed, lifted her grooming knife, and cut off the braid that denoted Aerise. She flung it onto the wine-soaked planks at Aerise's feet.

Finally, of all the adults, only her husband still faced her.

"How could you?" Duran murmured.

She knew when it had to have happened. That night in winter, when the person she thought was Duran, returning early from the sweat hut, slipped beneath the blankets without lighting the lamp. His body had been unusually warm, but this she took to be a byproduct of the steam.

"I was deceived," she murmured. "I thought it was you."

Duran's eyelids squeezed down tight. He nodded, chin trembling, and choked back a sob. But then he, too, turned away.

This was the worst. If her spouse had refused to believe her innocence, she could have hated him a little. The pain of losing him might then have pierced her less deeply. But to have him believe her and reject her anyway? That was as bitter as acorn meal before it has been leached.

No matter whether she had been raped or tricked, she was befouled. Now no person of Nine Vineyards would let her live among them.

A five-year-old boy—her own nephew, son of her eldest brother Nal—reached into one of the many buckets of stems and spoiled raisins that waited at the feet of the crowd and flung a handful at her. A second child did the same. Within moments, Aerise was being pelted.

She crouched, shielding her face. When she made no effort to move toward the door, some exchanged the raisins for clods of dirt. If she did not leave, eventually the barrage would consist of stones. At which point, the adults would join in the flinging.

Weeping, she fled the building.

She staggered as she crossed the threshold, but a sharp impact on her buttocks straightened her up. She lumbered on down the wagon way, past the cottages and lodges, out into the lanes of the vineyards. The rain of debris tapered off as parents called back their offspring. A few cruel whelps dogged her all the way into the woods.

Tripping and stumbling over roots the moon's weak light failed to reveal, she forged on until she could no longer hear the shouted threats. Only then, panting, her abdomen leaden and cramping, did she stop.

The trees loomed dark and close, hiding any sign that people lived nearby. This was the edge of her world, known to her only from forays to gather acorns or mushrooms. She had gone farther—to grind flour with the village women at the mill at Creekside, or to help her brothers and father sell wine at the fair at Traders Hollow—but never before had she been beyond the periphery of Nine Vineyards without at least one companion.

Her feet bled from the twigs she had landed on during her flight. Her throat ached from the crying, and from the dryness her panting had caused. But all her discomforts paled beside the shock of her exile.

She slapped her protruding belly. It made the babe kick, causing her to groan as her bladder received the impact, but she did it again. If the action forced her into labor, she welcomed it. Not that emptying her womb would change her fate. She was the cask that had produced vinegar, and would never be used for wine again.

She was not sure how long she raged, but by the time she was at last spent, fog had flowed in from the coast.

She had no shawl. Nor did she have a knife to cut fronds to build a shelter. She had nothing, in fact, but her cloak and the thin shift beneath it. She wormed into a thick patch of bracken she hoped would fend off a little of the mist. It was the only trace of comfort she found that night.

—o—

At last the sky lightened in the east. Aerise lay still, hoarding the warmth of the crushed bracken beneath her. For once, the baby was quiet. She had no desire to feel it squirm, knowing what it was.

She heard furtive footfalls along her trail and rolled up, reaching out in hope of finding a stout limb or a large stone to wield. Her hands were still empty when the intruder stepped into the strengthening light and she recognized her youngest sister.

Zana was carrying a bulging satchel. She set it down on the loam and rushed to Aerise's side —

And then stopped, not touching her. She eyed the glow of Aerise's belly. Carefully she approached again and laid a hand tentatively against Aerise's cheek.

Aerise kissed her sibling's hand. "Show me what you brought."

Zana produced four loaves of bread, two rounds of cheese, and both a skin and a hornflask of wine. Aerise's stomach rumbled at the sight of the food, but in the long run she knew she would be happiest to have the vessels, because after the wine was consumed, they could be refilled with water.

Zana jiggled the satchel. "There is a knife and a tinder box and a comb. I am sorry it is so little." They both knew there could be no more than one exchange. If Aerise lingered near the village, she would be hunted down.

"It could be worse. Winter could already be here." Aerise tore off a piece of a loaf and began wolfing it down. She made no attempt at finesse; with the awakening of the child's magic had come a fierce hunger.

Zana reached into the satchel and drew out one more item, a small, lidded urn. Butter. Aerise gratefully spread a thick smear on her bread, not attempting to ration it. It would only grow rancid if she hoarded it.

As Zana perceived just how much sustenance she required, new tears welled up to replace those she had already wiped away.

"Will it be enough to reach the enclave?" Zana asked.

"The enclave?"

"The Cursed Folk encampment. I am told it is all the way up near the headwaters this year."

"I would not know," Aerise said, stiffening.

Zana put her fingertips to her mouth, color filling her cheeks. "I did not mean —"

"Yes, you did." Aerise fought back new tears. "You believed I had made an arrangement. That I chose to be a broodwhore."

Zana looked away. She occupied her hands by helping restore the loaves to the satchel. The twitter of awakening sparrows in the branches grew loud.

"Promise me you will go there anyway," Zana said.

"I have no wish to see the one who did this to me, or his people."

Zana hiccupped. "You *must*. I want you to live, Aerise. I want you to live."

"I make no promises."

Zana knew that tone well. She fell silent.

"Go," Aerise said. "You've already risked too much to stay this long." If her absence from the village were discovered, she would be beaten severely.

Zana fled. All too soon, Aerise was again alone in the woods.

—o—

Over the next few days, as she slipped farther into the wild lands, Aerise tried to tell herself that she had meant what she implied to Zana—that she would rather die than seek out the Cursed Folk. Then, as the bread and cheese disappeared and real hunger set in, after the snuffling of a bear in the darkest part of the second night made her wet the seat of her shift in fright, after ants attacked the satchel and cheated her of the crumbs of her rations, she acknowledged that all along she had been following the course of the river toward its source, the place Zana had spoken of.

The susurrus of the stream filtered through the underbrush. Here it was a creek rather than a river, often flowing over stones and fallen logs, no longer the quiet waterway that flowed past her home. She made her way down into the gentle ravine and followed the animal trail that ran beside the stream.

Bruises aching, she clambered slowly over boulders and padded listlessly around tangles of vegetation. In early afternoon she stopped at a cave to rest, only to fall asleep on its soft sand bottom. The nap cost her too much of her remaining daylight and she was forced to spend the night there.

The next day, as she plodded up steepening slopes and the creek dwindled to a brook, she searched for some sign of the Cursed Folk. Even they could not inhabit an area without leaving evidence of their activities. But she saw only deer tracks, spent feathers, fox scat, the cast-off husks of caddis flies.

Finally her way was blocked by a short cliff. A spring welled up at its base, supplying the stream with much of its volume. Whatever sources of water lay above barely generated a dribble down the terraces of the cliff. These were the headwaters.

Zana had been wrong. The Cursed Folk were not here.

Hunger gnawed at her so desperately it made her sway. The needs of the child were overriding the disinterest in food that usually came with the second or third day of fasting. She limped back downsteam. Earlier in the day she had spotted a nettleberry bush on a high bank. She clawed her way up to it and gathered what the plant had to offer. She could see that foraging bears had stripped away the bulk of the crop, but she managed to harvest two handfuls.

She had to peel open the hairy rinds. The itchy filaments lodged in her thumbs. Despite the fruit's ripeness the squirts of pulp on her tongue were so bitter they puckered her mouth. She had only ever enjoyed nettleberry as an ingredient of jam. The tiny repast only served to intensify the hollowness in her midsection. She turned over a rock and found a fat grub and wolfed it down. That only made her feel as if something were writhing at the bottom of her gullet.

Her shift caught on a broken branch on her way down the embankment, ripping the fabric so that her bare belly showed through the opening, right where she would see it every time she looked down. The sight drained away what little of her dignity she had preserved until then.

Going downhill taxed her nearly as much as climbing, because pregnancy stole her sense of where her weight was balanced. She barely kept on long enough to reach a place where the ravine flattened and permitted the stream to spread itself out and grow still. Sunlight puddled across the surface as she waded along the pool's edge to a flat boulder. Tadpoles urgently hid themselves in the clouds of silt her feet disturbed.

Aerise lowered herself to her resting spot with effort. She sighed, too spent even to dip her fingers to try to rinse the sticky nettleberry juice from her hands. She did manage to slip the satchel from her shoulder.

Her womb contracted. She knew the sensation, having been through the process of birth twice already. She tried to calm her breathing. One twinge might signify little. She estimated she was not due for another fortnight, but she could not be sure given the stresses she had been put through, or given the half-breed nature of the child. By dawn she might be lying here, spent from labor, the birthing blood attracting wolves she could not defend herself from.

The baby stirred. A sharp kick made her gasp. Looking at her belly in anger, she was startled to see that the glow was no longer steady. The light was pulsing. At its brightest, it matched the level she had become accustomed to over the past few days. At its dimmest, she could not make it out in the daylight.

Then it faded altogether.

Fingers trembling, she pulled the torn edges of the hole in her shift wider apart. The taut skin of her abdomen was its normal hue. The baby's urgent shifting had eased. She could tell it was still wakeful, but its movements were now gentle—a subtle tickling.

She could not help but think of her firstborn, how he would fuss in her arms, only to be soothed and fall asleep when Duran picked him up and nestled him.

Aerise checked right and left. Then down. The sheen on the surface of the pool included a manlike outline.

Her heart began drumming. A shadow man was lying submerged in the water, apparently devoid of the need to breathe. So insubstantial was he that the current did not alter his position. Even minnows and tadpoles passed through him. He might have placed himself there—no, *must* have placed himself there—even before she had arrived.

Awkwardly she tottered to her feet—pretending to be even clumsier than she actually was, to conceal the moment when her hand slipped into the satchel and found the knife Zana had brought, which she hid behind her back as she rose.

He rose up as well. His form began to lose its ghostliness.

She knew it was the man who had raped her. Tall, fair-skinned, sparsely bearded, he looked enough like Duran she no longer blamed herself for being fooled in the unlit bedchamber that night. He would also have used sorcery to cloud her mind, of course.

He was naked. Aerise had not expected that, though she had been told that Cursed Folk could not bring their clothing with them when they slipped back and forth between planes of existence. Seeing him displayed in such a way made the mash of nettleberry in her stomach want to come back up.

Rivulets trickled down the muscled flesh of his body. The river sloshed and gurgled around his thighs. Suddenly he was very much a part of the world. Aerise did not waste a moment—she vaulted forward, thrusting the knife as her brother had taught her, low from her waist level, toward his gut. She committed to the leap, not caring how she landed as long as the knife reached him.

At the last instant he faded to mist. She plunged right through him, flopping into the water, which was just deep enough beyond him to receive her. She bounced off the stream bottom, bobbed back to the surface, and stumbled inelegantly to her feet, calf-deep in the midst of the pool.

She whirled about. The man was on the granite slab she had vacated. He solidified once more, taking two further steps back as he did so. He wiped the front of his torso. Blood seeped one drop at a time from a pinprick cut below his breastbone.

If she had been a moment faster, the blade would have penetrated him while he was corporeal. She had the satisfaction of seeing him realize how close he had come to being killed. She had the misery of knowing she had failed.

He was too far off now to surprise him again, in part a byproduct of how recklessly she had flung herself at him. But the knife was still in her hand, and there was one thing left she could do. She raised the weapon up, tip pointed straight at her womb.

The shadow man grew very still. She adjusted her slippery palm on the hilt, wrapping her other hand around the first, breathing so fast she was almost panting. His brow furrowed. In the alders, a squirrel peered at them, tail twitching. A frog sprang from the leaf litter into the creek. In the distance, a hawk uttered a territorial screech.

He did not rush at her, trying to overpower her. He did not plead. He simply waited.

Her grip loosened. The knife fell, splashed, and sank out of sight.

She dropped to her knees in the silt and pebbles. Water rode over her folded legs. She pulled at her hair until the pain in her scalp provoked the tears she needed. She was otherwise already drained of tears.

She could imagine all too well what she looked like at that moment—wet, bedraggled, nettleberry juice staining her chin. Wretched.

"Why?" she wailed. "Why did you do this to me? Why thrust your seed into me and not a broodwhore? Did it please you to deceive me?"

His expression contorted with such anguish her eyes widened. She stopped yanking her hair.

"It pleased me not." His accent and phrasing were archaic. "I did as I must. I did it for her." He pointed to her belly.

The glow reappeared.

She put her hand on the bulge. "Her? You can tell it's a girl?"

"Yes. And healthy she is. As I had hoped." A smile blossomed for an instant, quelled again as he continued to study her.

"The price you paid was high. I am in your debt." He reached out to her. "Will you come with me?"

He said it as if she had a choice. She did not accept his help in rising, but she nodded, and when he led the way, she followed.

—o—

The enclave lay far into the forest. It was well clear of the headwaters, the man explained, so that if raiders were sent to burn them out, they would not be found where rumor indicated. His folk avoided the river unless their sentry enchantments revealed the approach of a visitor they wished to contact. Sometimes this was a woman seeking to become a broodwhore. Usually it was a trader, come to parley for goods such as only the Cursed Folk made.

They stopped when they came to a fine old blood cedar. The man reached into a niche at the tree's base and pulled out a maternity gown. It was woolen—the fabric a product of spindle and loom. He held it out to her.

Because it came from him, she nearly refused it, but the prospect of being able to cover herself better overcame her distaste. Much to her relief, while she put the article over her torn shift, he donned an ensemble of deerskin and otter pelt, finally concealing his bare skin.

The rest of the journey required three long hours of hiking, their pace hindered by her exhaustion. Finally Aerise noticed the signs of habitation she had looked for earlier—a reduced quantity of deadfall branches due to the gathering of firewood, a hint of woodsmoke on the breeze, and then actual footprints on the trail.

Near dusk they reached the edge of a large meadow. Where the trees resumed on the other side she spotted a series of tents as well as an arbor roofed with cattail and fern thatch. She saw no more than thirty Cursed Folk, half of whom were children.

The meadow was soft even this late in the season, making her work to take each additional step. Aerise sighed and rubbed her lower back. "Is it much farther to the main encampment?"

"This is the main encampment," he said. "We do not gather in groups larger than this, or we would invite a scourging."

It was the second time he had spoken of the possibility of a raid. "How often does *that* happen?" she scoffed, recalling how successfully he had avoided her knife thrust. Who would bother attacking an enemy who could not be hurt?

"Often enough," he replied. "Our memories are long."

Aerise supposed it would be annoying to lose structures and possessions. Everything she saw up ahead was either portable or easily replaced. It was comforting to think her people could inflict some sort of pain upon his.

By the time they were two-thirds of the way across the meadow, the majority of the inhabitants of the enclave had still barely glanced in their direction. Aerise thought it eerie that the children would take so little notice. Then she recalled the stories.

"How long *are* your memories?" she asked.

"We age no more than one year for every ten that pass."

These then were not children like any she had seen. They had lost the boundless inquisitiveness of the very young. Only the babies were her juniors. Of them, there were two. Both were nursing at the breasts of women sitting beneath the arbor. These women, and a third who sat with them, gave off a different aura than everyone else present.

Broodwhores.

The group regarded Aerise intently. Their gazes kept returning to her swollen belly. The scrutiny made the fine hair on the back of Aerise's neck stiffen. They thought she was like them! They assumed she had made the same choice they had.

Two other women—these movingly fluidly, at home in their environment—strode past the arbor and met Aerise and her escort at the edge of the enclave. One appeared to be only a little older than Aerise, and like her had hair that tended toward coiled. The other possessed subtle lines by her eyes and traces of grey speckled her hair, which was merely wavy, like that of the man.

"This is Cloud," the man said, and the older woman inclined her head. "And this is Fern. They will be the mothers of the child you bear."

Aerise blinked. Much as she did not want to think of herself as the child's mother, it took her aback to hear anyone else described as such. "Both of them?"

"It is our way. Go with them now. If you require me, you have only to ask."

"And whom do I ask for?"

"You may call me Morel."

Her brows rose. "You are named after a mushroom?"

"The morel is my favorite treat. We do not share our true names with one of the Uncursed."

He walked on toward the heart of the encampment. Two elderly men and a woman met him there and ushered him into the large central tent. Aerise's eyes remained narrowed until the flap fell and he was lost to view.

When her attention returned to her escorts, she found both of them gazing at her coldly.

"You do not deserve the honor he bestows," Cloud said.

"I did not ask for it."

"Is it pity you seek? Pity us, who can only be mothers through the likes of you. Now come along. We have prepared a repast for you. Eat before you swoon from hunger. If we must needs shove food down your gullet while you sleep to keep our baby fed, we will not shrink to do so."

—o—

Modest as the Cursed Folk dwellings were compared to the sturdy buildings of Nine Vineyards, the tent Cloud and Fern thrust Aerise into was no hovel. It had four poles and enough headroom to easily stand straight. It even featured a lidded privy hole at the far end.

A roasted partridge, a kettle of porridge, and fresh greens waited on a stand made of interlaced forest twigs. Aerise set about devouring it at once, embarrassed at her directness but too ravenous to do otherwise.

While Aerise ate, Fern lit a large three-wicked candle to stave off the deepening twilight. Cloud unrolled and set up a trio of cots.

"That one." Aerise pointed. Her companions did not object.

Within moments, food gone, Aerise was clambering onto the one she had chosen. She fell asleep moments after Fern covered her with a fur blanket.

At first her slumber was deep, but with a baby pressing upon her bladder, it was inevitable she stirred. She saw to her needs quickly and returned to her cocoon of warmth as fast as she could. Only afterward did she realize she was not alone as she had thought. Fern was lying on the farthest cot, so much in the other realm only her outline showed.

Fern seemed to be almost levitating upon the bed. She was unclothed—Aerise understood the woman had no choice but to be unclothed. She showed no reaction to the night's chill. Aerise checked for some further attribute of alienness. Hoofed feet. A tail. Perhaps the absence of a navel. But Fern did not look meaningfully different than any young woman of Nine Vineyards that Aerise had ever shared the sweat lodge with.

Some time later, Aerise was briefly awakened again by the noise of the tent flap lifting. Cloud entered. Aerise feigned unconsciousness, but watched from beneath the fur.

Cloud undressed by simply turning to her phantom form and letting her garments fall. As she leaned over the candle she solidified again for a moment to have the force of wind to blow out the flames. For a moment the nearness of the illumination accentuated the detail of her body. Cloud's bosom rode as high on her chest as a maiden's. Her lower belly, between the wide hips so well configured for the birthing of children, bore no stretch marks.

—o—

In the morning, Fern and Cloud showed they meant their

pledge to see that the baby was well fed. Before Aerise had been awake more than a few moments, Cloud was setting down milk and eggs and more porridge in front of her.

Aerise was perfectly willing to cooperate with that particular duty. It was different when Fern ducked under the flap carrying a bucket of steaming water.

"What's that for?" Aerise asked.

"We will bathe you," they said.

"I'm clean enough for now."

The two women moistened rags in the hot water and wrung them out. "Strip," Cloud said.

"No," Aerise said. She stood and folded her arms. At full height she loomed over her hosts.

Cloud cleared her throat. "We are smaller and weaker than you, it is true. But if you do not yield, we will call in some of our menfolk to hold you down, and we will bathe you anyway."

Aerise had known Cloud only a matter of hours, but she could already tell the woman did not make empty threats. Sighing, she slipped out of her clothes.

Little did she imagine what the shadow women meant by "bathe." They scrubbed her until her skin was red.

"How many times are you going to do that?" Aerise objected when Fern lifted her arm wipe an area she had already attacked more than once.

"If we are to share this tent, we don't want to smell your stench."

Aerise's jaw dropped. She prided herself on her grooming. "Well, that's easy enough to deal with. I don't want to share a tent with you. If my odor bothers you, put me with the broodwhores."

Cloud tipped Aerise's chin until they were gazing straight at one another. "Morel requires that we look after you. But while we are leashed to one another, Fern and I decide what we will and will not endure."

"Do I really smell that bad to you, or do you just enjoy tormenting me?"

"Every night we fade. Our lice, our fleas, and the dirt and sweat on our bodies stay behind when we cross to the dream realm. We start each day fresh. This is the standard you will observe."

But having said that, Cloud wrung out her cloth and nodded to Fern, who did the same.

"I take it I am fresh enough now?" Aerise quipped.

"We are weary. This will have to do."

Aerise threw her gown on, picked up the bucket, stepped outside, and heaved the water away. She turned to confront Cloud and Fern as they emerged.

She held up the bucket. "Where do you heat the water?"

The two women shared a glance. "We do not," Fern said. "We get it from the hot spring in the meadow."

"Tomorrow, I will rise early and fill the bucket, and I will bathe myself. I am sure I will meet your standard."

Cloud gave another of her infuriating shrugs. "May it be so."

A deep male voice sounded just behind her, making Aerise jump. "I see you have recovered some of your strength."

Aerise spun. It was Morel.

"And some of her spirit," Cloud added.

Aerise scowled at them both, wishing she had not yet emptied the bucket so that she had water to fling at each of them.

"Is there aught I can provide?" Morel asked.

"You can leave me alone," Aerise replied.

He pursed his lips. He gazed steadily at her. She glared back. Finally he gave her a short bow.

"As you wish," he said.

She blinked. "Truly?"

"Until the child comes, I will leave you be." He strode off. He did not look back.

Aerise found herself the subject of another round of Fern and Cloud's cold stares. "You are the poorer for your choice," Cloud said. Then she added, less harshly, "But it is better this way, I think. Clearer."

—o—

Morel did as he had said. Over the next few days, Aerise only saw him from a distance. He usually remained in the encampment—Cloud assured her he would never be far away while she might go into labor. His tent stood near the center of the enclave, beside that of the elders. Young as Morel seemed to be— gradually Aerise came to understand that among his people, he was no further along than she was among her folk—he seemed to hold considerable status.

Her efforts at cleansing each morning were enough to save her from the humiliation of having Cloud and Fern handle her. The women dropped enough insults to imply they might have to take over, but she knew they were happy to be spared the task.

It was not long before Aerise began to appreciate the benefits of the ritual. The Cursed Folk really were astonishingly clean and well-groomed. Even the children began each day without grubby hands or feet. Their nostrils had no caked mucus. In the whole camp, only the broodwhores failed to maintain the same level of hygiene. Aerise saw the looks of contempt they received.

As the final stretch of her pregnancy wound down, Aerise spent much of each day outside in the open air, trying to stay cool. She observed many small examples of alienness. Children slipped in and out of their corporeal state as they ran about. Small enchantments kept candles burning longer than they should, made mosquitoes stay away. Yet to her surprise, for the most part the Cursed Folk lived their lives as anyone would. They prepared meals. They gathered firewood. They talked. They laughed.

"You are more like my own people than I was led to believe," Aerise said as she sat in the open with Cloud and Fern, digesting a meal of brook fish and spiced acorn mash.

"Are we not all children of the First Man and First Woman?" Cloud asked.

"No. How could it be so?"

Cloud clucked her tongue. "We were one great tribe until a small group of fools sought out the god of dreams. All who descend from them bear the legacy of that misstep. If we were so different, could Morel have gotten a child upon you?"

"I have not heard this tale before."

"Your people have chosen not to tell it. When we remind you we are related, we are disbelieved. Nevertheless we are as you would be if you were continually swept in and out of the dreamgod's realm. You would never be a natural mother, because no child quickens in a womb that does not remain in the solid world for nine months."

"I see." Aerise slid her hand along the bulge of her belly. "Are you telling me then that I would condone rape?"

Cloud folded her arms over her chest. "Is it rape when it is a not a product of depravity, but one of necessity?"

"Yes," Aerise replied unequivocally. "But I suppose you and I will never agree."

"Indeed. We never shall."

"Morel had other means open to him. Why did he choose as he did, if not for lust?"

Cloud grunted. It almost sounded like laughter, but Aerise suspected it was astonishment. "Look at yourself. Look at them."

The "them" the shadow woman pointed to were the broodwhores, sitting beneath their arbor as they usually did. Aerise had seen them every day, but she looked at them anew. The three women were unlike anyone else in the camp. They did not smile. Their sole activity, aside from suckling the babies, seemed to be endless rounds of runesticks, often punctuated by accusations of bungled castings. All three were marred in some way—awkward posture in one, a huge chin on another, pocked skin on the third. And of course, the sort of common dirtiness Cloud and Fern had demanded Aerise rid herself of.

Aerise, on the other hand, had smooth, well-complexioned skin. Her frame was solid and her flesh abundant, her hips wide, her eyesight keen. She had no birthmarks, no large moles, no warts. Duran had called her beautiful. He was biased, but even her rivals among the young women of Nine Vineyards had granted that had no need to feel humbled by either her body or her countenance.

She was the sort of woman a man selects when he wants to choose a mate to bear his children. The broodwhores were...dregs.

Cloud had just tendered her a compliment. Aerise wished she

did not deserve it. If she had been less appealing, she would not be where she was.

—o—

The baby came right on time, a fortnight after her arrival. Feeling contractions in the middle of the night, Aerise awakened Fern and Cloud. Experience told her she had hours to go yet, but if she were going to be sleepless, she wanted them to share the misery.

As midwives, her companions were well schooled. They took her to a lean-to at the meadow's edge, where they had plenty of clean, hot water close at hand. They helped her walk back and forth to speed things along, get her water to break. They reminded her when to push, and when to breathe.

She sent her mind elsewhere when the agony reached a crescendo. She came back to full consciousness when the pressure between her legs abruptly eased, and a newborn's cry resounded through the forest. She opened her eyes. Cloud was cleaning the baby's face. She lowered the girl to Aerise's bosom. Fern lay a light blanket atop them while the older woman turned her attention to the umbilical cord and the delivery of the afterbirth.

The baby continued to wail. "Shhhhhh," Aerise said, holding its head gently against her chest, snug enough to be near the reassuring thump of her heartbeat. The little one calmed down.

Aerise gazed at the tiny hand, the tiny mouth, the shiny eyes. She tried hard to find some fault, some aspect she could recognize as Cursed and therefore hate, but she failed.

—o—

Even after the arrival of the baby, Morel remained clear of

Aerise as much as possible, letting Cloud and Fern be his intermediaries, but he did not avoid his little daughter. He played with her, swayed her to sleep, let her nap in the crook of his neck. Aerise realized he was spending more time with the baby than she herself. The foster parents were loathe to let her take possession of the child at all save for feedings.

One afternoon, three weeks after the birth, Cloud suddenly announced, "You may leave tomorrow, if you wish."

Aerise's head jerked up so abruptly it jostled the baby off the nipple. "What?" she asked, restoring things before the young one fussed.

"It is customary that a broodmother weans the baby before her service is done," Cloud said. "But Morel bids us set you free if you desire. The broodwhores can serve as wetnurses."

"Or you can stay until next summer begins," Fern said. "And in so doing, earn a greater reward."

Leave? Aerise hesitated. Part of her wanted to leap to her feet and scamper off toward whatever future awaited. But where could she go? The nights were growing crisp. The forest held no more welcome than it had the first time. She had not yet made a plan.

"If Morel had not insisted, would you have made me this offer?"

Cloud and Fern glanced at one another, then back to Aerise. "No," Cloud admitted. "We pled the needs of the child. A mother's milk is best."

Aerise stroked the baby's cheek. The tug at her breast was strong and regular, a bittersweet reminder of the time not so long ago when her second-born had nursed in her arms just that way, before the bog fever swept the village, first stealing away the appetite of the child and then taking her life, along with the life of her toddler brother.

"I will stay," Aerise replied.

Fern actually smiled. Cloud let out the breath she had been holding.

"You truly thought I would leave?" Aerise asked, as if she had not been tempted.

"Your anger is deep," Cloud said.

Aerise nodded. "So it is. But none of what was done to me was *her* choice." She lifted the baby up and gave her a little kiss before cradling her in the crook of her neck to burp her.

Cloud lifted the tent flap. Morel was standing twenty paces away. Cloud gestured in the sign-talk the Cursed Folk used when they were insubstantial and incapable of producing sound from their throats. Morel's expression brightened. He gazed at Aerise long and appreciatively.

"Close the flap," she demanded. Cloud sighed, but obeyed.

—o—

The months passed. The baby thrived. When frost whitened the forest floor, the Cursed Folk moved their camp to an even more remote area, where the game was less wary of hunters and meat would be plentiful through the cold months. Snow fell thrice and it stuck to the ground longer than Aerise was used to from living nearer the coast. The Cursed Folk tents remained extraordinarily warm and snug, demonstrating the enchantments upon them.

Aerise never felt as though she were a member of the enclave. The denizens did not seek her out, nor invite her to join their games of chance or storytelling circles. Even the baby's presence could not meaningfully assuage her loneliness. But her turmoil remained at a simmer. She bickered less with Cloud and Fern. She deigned on rare occasions to mutter a few words to Morel or even accept the child directly from his arms when she cried to be suckled. She was made comfortable and kept well fed in all the ways that would keep her milk both good and abundant. The days blended together until an afternoon when birds were nest-building in the trees and mushrooms were sprouting thickly on rotted logs. It was the day the broodwhores left.

Aerise was watching from her favorite nursing spot, a long flat log near which Cloud and Fern had pitched the tent. The matriarch of the Cursed Folk met with the broodwhores in the center of the encampment. She handed the one with the pocked skin a phial containing a winedark liquid, which the woman quickly secreted away in a pouch of her cloak.

The other younger women received a purse made of deerskin. The woman immediately untied the drawstrings and upended it. A cascade of silver coins and copper bits dropped into the lap of her skirt. Counting, the woman restored the money to the purse.

"The Mother's Bounties," Aerise said.

"Yes," Cloud confirmed.

"Why do you give that one money? Why not a potion like the other? Did you find her service poor?"

"She served adequately. She wanted nothing magical. She chose thus the first time, and now wishes she had not."

Aerise hesitated. "The first time?"

"She bore a child for members of our enclave two years ago. The baby died of a pox when it was not yet weaned, but that was not the mother's fault, and so we honored the pact. At her request we gave her a snare otters would find irresistible. Her folk are fur trappers and she imagined she would rise high in their favor. Instead they recognized what she must have done to acquire such a treasure, and cast her into exile. They kept the charm, of course. I'm told they had good luck gathering pelts this past season."

"She spun you a tale," Aerise replied. "Her own kin would not treat her so."

"Did she cut off her own ears, then?"

Aerise jumped. Something about the broodwhore's features had always been disturbing. Cringing, Aerise finally perceived how the hair that the woman always kept down along the sides of her head hung too freely, without flaring around earlobes as it should. All at once she recalled the words shouted after her as she fled the village, telling her how lucky she was to be leaving with her skin intact.

"I never told you, did I, that the strain of yeast that makes the wine of your village so remarkable was once a Mother's Bounty."

"You lie," Aerise said, but her voice barely rose above a whisper.

"Your village was founded only three centuries ago. I was a girl when that sorcery was cast. I could introduce you to the man who wrought it, if you wish, though 'twould require us to journey to the next enclave to the south."

Aerise searched for a way to disbelieve what she was hearing, but all she could think was how many times she had heard, from her own people and from everyone at the fair at Traders Hollow, how the vintages of Nine Vineyards consistently surpassed those made anywhere else in the region.

"If she spun us a tale, it was one we had heard before. The Uncursed are glad enough to own and benefit from our creations, but the mothers themselves are condemned for consorting with us. This woman takes coin because she can conceal how she obtained it. Maybe she will be more fortunate this time. She knows to seek out a life where her face is not known, and spend the money a little at a time, never revealing how much she has in reserve."

The broodwhores shouldered their packs and set off upslope. Aerise guessed they would try to join a settlement of the Shepherd Folk on the other side of the range. The older woman, the one who had never served as a wetnurse during the whole time Aerise had lived in the enclave, trailed after the other two.

The latter had received no reward. Cloud anticipated Aerise's question and said, "She was paid long ago. Her childbearing years have passed, but we let her stay as long as the others were here. But when you leave us, we will move the camp again. We will accept no new broodwhores until we are reestablished."

It was the first time in many weeks she had made reference to Aerise's leavetaking. Aerise studied the fretful, tentative pace of the trio as they vanished among the trees. The one whose ears had been cut off looked back four times before she passed out of sight.

—o—

One evening, as twilight lingered far into the night and the warmth of the day clung like a garment, the baby suddenly felt light in Aerise's embrace, and the tug at her nipple vanished. All at once the child...faded. She slipped right out of Aerise's grip and out of her swaddling clothes and tumbled to the floor, landing silently. She lay there on her back, arms and legs waving, clearly wailing in surprise but producing no audible noise. Her form was misty— nearly transparent.

Fern transformed into her ghostly state, her clothes falling away. She picked the baby up, and held her close. Soon the baby stopped crying. A smile brightened her little face. Fern began playing their favorite game of pat-hands. She obviously—though silently—giggled when Fern swept her through a tent pole, and she passed right through.

"It is almost time for you to go," Cloud told Aerise.

"I know," Aerise murmured.

—o—

In the next fortnight, the people of the enclave packed their belongings and moved away. On the final morning, friends took away Fern and Cloud's tent. Aerise was left sitting on her familiar log, nursing the child one last time while Fern, Cloud, and Morel waited by the central firepit, where the storytelling circle and elders' councils had been held for the past season.

Gradually the baby finished feeding. She burbled in contentment. She was eating solid food regularly now, and had only been nursing lightly once in the morning and once in the evening, sometimes indifferently. Aerise was glad to see her indulging in the experience this time.

Suddenly Fern was looming above them, naked and ghostly. The baby cooed and slipped into the dreamgod's realm. The swaddling clothes went limp and collapsed on Aerise's lap. Fern picked up her foster child and rejoined Cloud, who remained solid, carrying Fern's attire and the baby's necessities.

They did not say a word of farewell to Aerise. She said none to them. Within moments they were ambling off through the trees. They were soon lost to view. Morel alone remained.

Tears poured down Aerise's face. She stood up, as if to follow, but knowing it was not a choice open to her. "I don't even know her name," she murmured. She lifted a corner of her nursing vest to wipe her eyes. The aroma of her infant wafted into her nose.

Morel's voice was strangely husky. "There is only one thing left. The Mother's Bounty."

"So I am a broodwhore after all."

"A debt is owed. Simply that." He lifted the swaddling clothes that had fallen from her lap to the ground. Smelled them. "And more. I swore that if you grieved at this parting, I would grant to you whatever boon was within my power to create."

She opened her mouth. He raised a warning finger. "Anything save vengeance."

"Give me a life as fine as what you took," she snapped. "A life among my people. In my own village."

She meant it as a challenge—a demand he could not fulfill, which would put the lie to his sincerity. It was only when she looked up and saw the numb contemplation on his face that she even imagined her request might be possible to grant. Abruptly she sat back down on the log.

"What you ask..." He blanched. "To have any hope, you must take great risks. Are you willing to do what is necessary?"

Her breath had vanished so fully she could hardly get the words out. "Do you toy with my hopes? To have *that*? I will do whatever I must."

He rubbed his neck like a man facing the ordeal of his life. "If after I have told you the whole of it, your answer is the same, then our bargain is sealed."

—o—

The first thing Aerise was aware of was the dustiness in her throat. She coughed.

Someone lifted her head up. The rim of an earthenware cup was pressed to her lips. She drank without opening her eyes, without truly coming awake. The second cup smelled of honey, anise, and something fiery. No sooner had she gulped it down than her bid for consciousness failed.

And so it went, how many occasions she could not say. Eventually she awoke fully. For the first time she managed to open her eyes and knew where she was. The stone vault of the cavern loomed over her. Light seeped in where the boulder sealing the entrance had been removed.

Morel leaned near, supported her head again, and served another draught of his potion. Gradually her eyes were able to focus. His countenance had changed. Fine lines had deepened where the skin had formerly been smooth.

"How...long?" she coughed.

"Sixty years. It will have to serve. I dared not leave you longer."

"Let me see," she said as she grasped the meaning of his statement.

He gently lifted her arm in front of her face. Where a plump hand and generous forearm had been, what she saw now was a crone's—no, a mummy's—desiccated appendage, looking as crusted and grey as she felt inside.

"The rest," she insisted.

He hesitated, seemed about to argue, but gradually he peeled back the blanket, unveiling her body. She tried to lift her head to view it, but could not until he assisted her.

She was speechless at the sight. When she had been lowered to the slab, her milk-laden breasts had perched heavily on her ribcage. Now they were empty, nippled flaps of skin. Her belly dipped lower than she could see from her angle, the hipbones rising like mountain peaks on the other side. Her legs seemed to be little more than bones overlaid with dried skin. She suspected the odd nest of coils by her feet were the remains of toenails Morel had recently trimmed away.

Aerise fought to contain her horror. He had told her it would be this way when he sealed her in this subterranean chamber. He had also said that, as long as she did not perish altogether, her body would ultimately have suffered no lasting harm.

"Drink," he said. "Drink and drink, then drink again. This will all change, and seem but a dream."

Surely he was a liar. But she did as he said.

—o—

On the day Aerise and Morel journeyed to Nine Vineyards, her muscles were strong enough to help load the sacks of feed for the oxen. Her complexion had deepened from pallid to lightly tanned. She did not fill her new clothes as amply as she had her old ones, and she still craved twice as much water per day as normal, but as the shadow man had promised, her health was sound. She no longer doubted she would finish the recovery as he indicated—in a year or two, she would have her curves back, her cheeks would be rosy, and her hair would reclaim its bounce. In six decades of hibernation, she had in fact aged only three years.

She inhaled sharply as they rounded a bend and she caught her first glimpse of the village. Nine Vineyards had grown during her time away. The headman's house was now a stone manse three stories high, with a watchtower. A ferry sat at anchorage on the river bank where the smokehouse had been, and a newer, larger smokehouse stood a hundred paces upstream. A huge warehouse had been recently built beside the winery. The latter improvement provided the means to their goal. More wine and more storage space mean more barrels were needed, and someone had to construct those barrels.

"You are the new cooper?" asked the head vintner as Morel tugged back on the reins and brought his wagon and team to a halt.

Morel gestured at the piles of staves and strap in the rear of the wagon. "At your service."

"Let me show you your workshop," the vintner said.

Morel held up a hand. "If you please, my wife would like to see the quarters you've arranged. We took the long road getting here. She is very tired."

"Ah. Of course. Follow me."

Aerise's heart was beating fast as Morel helped her down from the wagon, but her spirits were high. Morel's command of modern vernacular, in which he had schooled himself these past decades, had not failed him. When he broadened a vowel or two to capture the accent of a denizen of Baymouth, the listener had believed him to be who he said he was.

The vintner led them to a cottage behind the winery. He opened the door for her. "I hope you will find this adequate."

When she reached the center of the main room, she turned in a slow circle, letting her eyes adjust. Fresh, tight thatch lay above the rafters. The floor showed no gouges and only a few stains. The dwelling was perhaps ten years old, not yet spoiled by the touches of those who had inhabited it thus far.

It smelled of home. Of wine vats stored near. Of the river. Of tilled soil. All the smells she had been deprived of in the Cursed Folk enclave.

She smiled. "Yes. Yes, it is adequate." She moved quickly to the larder, checked a crock to confirm it held cured olives, then began arranging space on the shelves for the goods from the wagon. She blew air to clear away dust and cobwebs—though in truth, the place showed every sign it had been well cleaned in anticipation of their arrival.

The vintner chuckled. "I will check back anon." He paused at the door. "Mind you don't exhaust yourself. Tomorrow night we will have festivities in the great lodge to welcome you. The whole village will be there."

She and Morel both caught their breaths.

"Is anything wrong?" the vintner asked.

Morel shrugged, appearing to make light of it. "My wife is somewhat shy. She was raised on a very small farm. But of course, we will be there."

"Good," the man said. He winked at Aerise. "I am sure you will enjoy yourself."

She smiled weakly. "I am sure I will."

After the man let himself out, Aerise went to the water basin, moistened her scarf, and wiped her suddenly hot face.

"If it would put you at ease, we could concoct an excuse," Morel suggested. "I could go alone."

She steadied herself. "No. That would only raise suspicions. We must both be there."

—o—

The great lodge was the same building in which Aerise's

banishment had taken place. A nave had been added to increase its capacity, but the main chamber assaulted her with memories. It took all her will not to tremble as she moved about beneath familiar soot-stained beams, awash in scents known to her from babyhood.

Morel endeavored to be the center of attention, laughing, telling stories, cheerfully greeting one and all. Aerise gravitated to the periphery, avoiding the full light, speaking only enough to observe good manners. She and Morel had rehearsed her feigned background as a daughter of a recently-deceased dairyman near Baymouth, but she uttered only the dull outline of this tale when asked about her origin, for fear her listeners would take an interest and gather around her to listen. It was not in her nature to be reticent; she had to still her tongue more than once when she found herself about to carry on.

Whenever possible, she avoided the elders. Sixty years was a long time, but not as long as she and Morel had aimed for when they made their pact. So short a span meant not all of the people she had known were dead. In the first few minutes she recognized three individuals whom she had known. She had last seen them as children who had flung stems and spoiled grapes at her to drive her from the village. Much as she wished to avoid it, she knew she must put their memories to the test. She let herself be introduced to each, and exchanged a few sentences. They showed no sign that they made any connection between the cooper's bony, reserved wife and the plump, boisterous Aerise of Nine Vineyards they had known. Gradually the tension in her lower gut began to ease.

At one point, revellers parted in such a way that Aerise could glance right across the room. She spotted a white-haired, wrinkled matron on a bench against the wall.

The old woman lacked teeth. Her jowls hung low. Her eyes—one of them clouded over with white—could scarcely be made out amid the puffiness of her face. But by the time the crowd shifted again and hid her from view, Aerise had identified her as Zana.

"Excuse me," Aerise told her nearest companions, and rushed out to the privy. She barely managed to shut herself in before she began sobbing. She managed to suppress the noise, but not the shuddering and tears.

When she was able to control herself, she wiped her face dry and reentered the lodge. Spine stiff as a wagon yoke, she continued to mingle. She did not go to the side of the room where Zana sat until several of the oldest folk, worn out early, made their exit—Zana among them, a pair of adolescent girls assisting her.

Aerise longed to follow. The desire tightened her throat so much she spoke in rasps for the rest of the evening.

—o—

That night Aerise tossed and turned. The bed, which had been so reassuring the night before, provided no comfort now.

"I cannot do it," she murmured aloud to herself. The pretense, the knowledge she would be dwelling near her favorite kinswoman and be forced to avoid her at every turn—it seemed too impossible, despite all she had gone through to get to this point. She had been a fool to ask for it. Had only done so because she wanted to punish Morel by asking for the impossible.

Enough. She would tell the shadow man, and make an end to it.

She rose and went into the main room of the cottage, where she had left him sleeping near the hearth. She had not been able to bring herself to let him share the bedroom, though to do otherwise carried the risk that some neighbor might notice clues and question whether they were truly husband and wife. Three steps within, she halted so quickly she nearly keeled over forward.

Morel was not simply lying there. He was writhing. His body twisted and bent, caught in paroxysms that distorted his shape in ways that would be impossible while he was in his solid form. Whether he was conscious or slumbering was unclear. While he thrashed, sometimes the glow of the embers fell on his face, and what she saw was a rictus, eyes squeezed shut, teeth showing. Muscles were bulging unnaturally all over his body.

"Morel!" she called. "Morel! Wake up!"

His eyes blinked open. All at once he shifted from misty to solid. As soon as he had completed the transition, he sucked in a desperate chestful of air. The breath seemed to quell the throes. The rictus subsided. Trembling, sweating, moaning, he tucked himself in a curl like a newborn.

"What happened to you?" she asked.

He coughed. She brought him a dipper of water. He tried to hold it, but his hand quivered too much. She took it back and tipped the serving into his mouth. He was calmer after he had swallowed.

"It happens most nights," he replied, voice sluggish and toneless. "All of my folk suffer unless they divide their existence between this realm and the other, never biding too long in either. Today, among so many witnesses, I tarried too many hours in only one."

"I had no inkling."

"It is not your concern. Do not trouble yourself. I endured much worse in Baymouth."

He referred to the period he had spent an apprentice cooper, learning the craft, establishing a history that would stand up to scrutiny if investigated by anyone from Nine Vineyards. He had dwelled in Baymouth four years.

"Worse than what I saw just now?" she asked.

"Yes. I had no one such as you to stand guard. An apprentice works long hours, with little privacy."

Aerise said nothing. She fetched another dipper of water.

He drank. "Did you come in for a reason? My struggles surely produced no clamor."

"No," she said quickly. "No, I couldn't sleep. I was simply... pacing. Pay me no mind." She retreated quickly into the bedroom and shut the door.

She lay back on her bed. Everything seemed so different than when she had been lying there minutes earlier. She could not say she was sorry that Morel endured such agony. In some ways, he could never experience enough to satisfy her. But if he could keep to the plan despite all that, if he had somehow found the fortitude not to break his vow and leave her in the cavern for eternity, then she would have to find the means to cope with her own anguish. To do otherwise would be to let him shame her all over again.

—o—

The next week was the worst of it. Aerise's heart would trip each time she glimpsed Zana or anyone similarly old. She limited the occasions she went out in public, using the excuse that she wanted to arrange the cottage to her liking. She accepted an invitation to a barrel tasting of the upcoming vintage, but only after determining that the attendees would only be workers and their spouses, all too young to have known her in the past.

Only on the seventh day did she dare to go to the one part of the village she had dreaded as much as craved to see. Checking regularly to be sure she was not observed, she approached the little house that she and Duran had shared. By now, having made a few careful, tangential queries, she had confirmed that Duran himself was dead, and she had learned what he had done with his life, once she had been erased from it.

The house had changed less than some in the village. Rather than expanding it as his family grew, Duran had built a second, larger structure that shared the same yard, and then expanded the latter, because he had fathered six children with his second wife, and in middle age served as stepfather to the three that came with the widow he married next.

The maple that had been a sapling cast thick shade over his grave. She did not go near it—someone might look out a window and see her—but she let her glance linger on the marker.

"Were you happy?" she asked the air. "Tell me my going did not steal your smile forever."

A beam of light glinted through a gap in the leaves and touched the gravestone. Yes, he had been happy, the omen said. He had been happy, said the fineness of the workmanship of the second house, the orderly nature of the yard, the number of descendants residing in the community. Whatever anguish had lingered—Aerise could not find enough generousness of spirit to hope he had known no regrets at all—had healed in time. It gave her a model to follow, if she could manage.

—o—

She could not have said, after the fact, just when she began to believe the scheme would succeed. Maybe it was as early as the first few weeks, when she ceased pretending to have a Baymouth accent—a part of the act that had never come easy—and spoke in her normal voice, and everyone accepted she simply had a good ear and had learned to mimic those around her. Maybe it occurred during the harvest, when she unconsciously joined in the singing of the classic village work chant, and no one thought it odd that a girl from a farm near Baymouth knew it, but just assumed she had heard it at some point in the months she had lived among them. Perhaps it happened in the winter, during the long sessions of storytelling in the great lodge, when one of her own nephews, now a wizened elder of seventy years, told the story of her banishment—never mentioning her by name, for that was forbidden, and never revealing the harlot had been someone he personally knew—and not one person in the circle glanced her way.

Then came the evening at the sweatlodge. She felt a hand fall on her shoulder. Startled, she turned. A crone was leaning near to peer closely at her face.

It was Zana.

Aerise's throat went dry. She had encountered her sister many times since the evening of the welcoming feast. Widowed for a fourth time, Zana lived behind the weaver's house, cared for by a loving clan of children, grandchildren, and great-grandchildren, and Aerise had seen her taking daily walks to the river. They had both attended village funerals, weddings, and storytelling circles. However, in all instances Aerise had endeavored to stay outside the range of Zana's compromised vision. They had never before been in the sweat lodge at the same time. Like most of the elderly women of Nine Vineyards, Zana typically visited the place in the early evening, and Aerise always arrived late.

But at last, it had happened. Zana's good eye had settled upon her while she was unaware. In the past six months, Aerise's body had filled out again, becoming replete with the abundance and comeliness that Zana had often said she wished she had more of.

Zana stared. Blinked. Stared again. And finally a tear crept down her face.

Aerise began to cry as well.

Zana sat on the bench beside her. "Throw a little more water on the rocks," she said.

Aerise scooped the dipper into the barrel and splashed the hot cobblestones, sending a new dose of steam into the lodge's interior. Zana inhaled deeply.

"Do you miss your old home, cooper's wife?" Zana asked.

"This is my home," Aerise replied softly. "This is the place where my happiness lies."

Zana nodded. A short time later the other women in the lodge happened to leave. When they were alone, Zana reached out and grasped her sister's hand.

They sat together, the sweat of their palms mingling.

—o—

Morel was waiting by the hearth when Aerise returned. She could tell he had assumed solid form a moment before, when he had heard her footsteps approaching. He wore only the blanket he had thrown over himself.

"I expected you ere now," he said.

"All is well," she said. "I believe the end of your service is nigh."

A brightness came into his eyes. It reminded Aerise of the

emotion he displayed whenever he bounced his daughter in his arms. She had not seen that gleam in all the three seasons they had dwelt in Nine Vineyards.

To her surprise, she wished he had showed a trace of wistfulness.

"Tell me," he said.

She told him of her encounter with Zana. When she was done, he nodded. "As you say. Soon you will be free of me, and I of you. Here is how I propose to do it."

They talked deep into the night.

—o—

A fortnight later, in the brightness of a springtime afternoon, a solemn knock resounded on the door of the cottage.

Aerise answered. Outside stood the vintner and the headman. Both hung their heads, avoiding eye contact, and shifted from foot to foot. The headman coughed. "Lady Cooper..."

"What has happened?" she asked with alarm.

"Your husband went fishing today at the rapids with a group..."

"Yes. I know."

The headman cleared his throat. "He slipped on a wet rock and fell in. He did not come back up. The men are still searching, but they have not found his body, but it has been too long now to hope. He...he has drowned."

Aerise let her face contort more and more with each word. When the headman said "drowned," she whirled, fell to her knees just inside the cottage, and pulled at her hair, wailing at the top of her lungs. The men hovered over her, trying to mutter condolences. She blocked them out, concentrating on her performance. Try as she might, she could not summon tears. She had not expected to. Not for him. But the rest of the act came surprisingly easy. She heaved and thrashed and wailed. They could not see her face to observe the lack of weeping, and they were only males. She knew they accepted her reaction as true grief.

And soon, so would the whole village.

—o—

The vintner told her she could stay in the cottage until the replacement cooper was hired, and assured her that would not be for many months. Out in the fields the grape canes had barely started to show green growth and the crush was months away. There were plenty of barrels on hand until then—the late cooper, the vintner remarked with appreciation, had been an industrious tradesman and had prepared plenty of stock.

Aerise had no fear that she would find new living arrangements by then. Though not with Zana. The one thing that might stir certain elders to recall one Aerise daughter of Makk would be a sudden acceptance of a Baymouth cooper's wife into the household of another daughter of Makk.

The only hardship remaining was that she was still obliged to drag about, pretending to mourn. It was many weeks before she allowed her step and posture to display the verve that churned within. As soon as she did so, village bachelors began "accidentally" crossing her path. They offered to do small favors for her, from repairing her hen coop or splitting fresh cord wood for her hearth, and bit by bit she said yes to some of these overtures, preparing food for them in exchange.

She judged it best to wait a year before she wed. But it was apparent that as far as the community was concerned, less than that would not be taken amiss.

—o—

She saw Morel only one more time. On midsummer night, she slipped away from the solstice celebration in the town center and made her way down to the river.

The moonlight on the water became the white gleam of his body, emerging. He did not come alone. Beside him rose a girl child, looking to be about seven years old. She was robust and round-cheeked like Aerise had been at that age—not lithe like her father.

Aerise held out her hands. The girl clasped them.

How warm her hands were. Full of life's vigor. Aerise gazed until the moon hid behind the leaves of a river alder, making her offspring's features too dim and ghostly—too much like what she was.

At the last, Aerise leaned in and gave her a kiss. She smiled.

Her daughter smiled back.

"My true name is Rahella," the girl said.

When they separated, Aerise was reminded of the moment the Cursed Folk foster mothers had cut the cord, that day she gave birth by the meadow. The severed parts would never be joined again. This was surely the last time she would ever see this child of her body.

Morel waited in the shallows. When the girl reached him, he cupped her chin. Seeing the tenderness of the gesture, aware of the pride in his eyes, Aerise could not hate him. Forgive him? No. But understand him? Yes. For him, it had not been enough to bring a child into the world. It needed to be a child as fine as Rahella.

The pair became intangible and walked off across the surface of the water. From time to time, until they slipped out of sight, Rahella turned to catch glimpses of her mother.

Finally Aerise climbed the bank and made her way along the river path to the village. It was not a short walk, but it seemed so.

No braids dangled from her head, tallying the number of her living offspring. She had no husband. For family she had only one aged sibling, not long for this world. But she had youth. She had time. And she had recovered her place.

She arrived back in the village murmuring a tune, and when the blacksmith's sons asked her to dance with them around the bonfire, jostling and nudging each other to be the first to twirl her around, she laughed and said yes.

ACKNOWLEDGMENTS

Cover art: "Cave of the Storm Nymphs" by Edward John Poynter, 1903.

"A Swain of Kneaded Moonlight" was first published in *The Feathered Edge: Tales of Magic, Love, and Daring*, edited by Deborah J. Ross. Copyright © 2012 by Dave Smeds.

"The Page Turner" was first published in *Marion Zimmer Bradley's Sword & Sorceress XXVI*, edited by Elisabeth Waters. Copyright © 2011 by Dave Smeds.

"The Beheaded Queen" was first published in *Lace and Blade*, edited by Deborah J. Ross. Copyright © 2008 by Dave Smeds.

"The Etherine Road" was first published in *Marion Zimmer Bradley's Sword & Sorceress XXV*, edited by Elisabeth Waters. Copyright © 2010 by Dave Smeds.

"A Morsel for the Plague Queen" was first published in *Marion Zimmer Bradley's Sword & Sorceress XXIII*, edited by Elisabeth Waters. Copyright © 2008 by Dave Smeds.

"The Vapors of Crocodile Fen" was first published in *Marion Zimmer Bradley's Sword & Sorceress XXIV*, edited by Elisabeth Waters. Copyright © 2009 by Dave Smeds.

"Bearing Shadows" was first published in *Marion Zimmer Bradley's Sword & Sorceress XXII*, edited by Elisabeth Waters. Copyright © 2007 by Dave Smeds.

www.ingramcontent.com/pod-product-compliance
Lightning Source LLC
Chambersburg PA
CBHW050527260626
47157CB00004B/1508